HUMAN FACTOR

Suddenly Finn's voice pierced the cabin's interior. Interference from the atmospheric sleeve caused the transmission to break up. "Gwen ... don't ... don't..."

Dirk watched Gwen's tortured expression out of the corner of his eye.

Without warning, she wrenched back on the stick. The nose reared; the ship bucked. And they were falling. There was no better word. Flat. The skuttle's wide beam, rather than her nose, pointed at the planet.

And they were spinning out of control!

The speaker exploded with sound. "Gwen, stop! Gwen! GWEN! NO-O-O-O!"

There was a muffled boom, and they were buffeted about. The skuttle rocked and pitched as their vehicle was completely engulfed in flames.

Also in the Point SF series:

HUMAN FACTOR

Jessica Palmer

■SCHOLASTIC

Scholastic Children's Books,
Commonwealth House, 1–19 New Oxford Street,
London WC1A 1NU, UK
a division of Scholastic Ltd
London ~ New York ~ Toronto ~ Sydney ~ Auckland

Published in the UK by Scholastic Ltd, 1996

Copyright © Jessica Palmer, 1996

ISBN 0 590 13385 3

Typeset by DP Photosetting, Aylesbury, Bucks.
Printed by Cox & Wyman Ltd, Reading, Berks.

10 9 8 7 6 5 4 3 2 1

For my sister, Katie,
gone for many years and found again at last

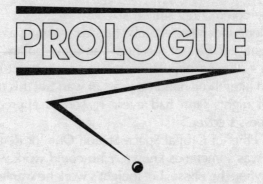

PROLOGUE

17/5/2334

O-SIX-TWENTY

ARE YOU SURE?

The commander of Orbital Space Station One, Perry Finn, stared at the question and swallowed hard. His Adam's apple bobbed up and down in his throat.

ARE YOU SURE?

The question winked at him incessantly.

Finn rubbed sweaty palms against his trousers, fished around in his pocket to extract a carrying case and counted the micro-diskettes within.

Ten. They were all here.

He typed *yes*, leaned back in his chair, kicked up his feet and cradled his head in twined fingers.

The computer's response was almost instantaneous.

FILES DELETED.

The commander smiled.

A lone incandescent tube burned, creating a cone of light. All part of the new "austerity policy", as Earth's starving population tried to reconstruct their world after three hundred years of war. But this night of all nights Finn had every reason to appreciate darkness's cover.

As chief of Orbital Space Station One, or Retrofit, as it was sometimes known, Finn could work when and where he chose, but tonight's work he wanted to remain unobserved or, failing that, unremarked. So he was glad of the "state of emergency", for no one would question him if they found him working under night's black mantle as policy and prudence demanded.

The fragile illumination was partially augmented by the glow of the terminal and the overhead screen that threw his face into relief, all planes and box-like chasms. The man paused to consider the view above his head where the blue ball of Earth pivoted slowly. At this distance the planet was featureless, a single ocean dotted with island clusters. All that was left of Earth's land masses.

The image completely filled the screen, like a sparkling sapphire. Remote ... breathtaking ... distant ... cold.

The view remained the same, even though the space station revolved in order to maintain an Earth-like gravitational pull of 3/4 G. The camera lens was positioned in such a way upon the central axis that the planet stayed stationary despite the orbital's spin.

With a sigh, Finn typed in the sequence that would link him to the Earth-side master computer, AWS, to repeat the process. Not a difficult manoeuvre, not as it had once been in those first bleak days immediately after the Galactic Conflict when the system had refused to interface with any human besides the youth, Dirk Alexander. The very same Dirk Alexander who had revealed the war for what it was. A lie.

There was no war, never had been really. The conflict was a carefully maintained fiction, created solely to provide an industrial base for the water-logged world. Neither were there "sides". No good guys or bad guys. No enemy. No human soldiers. Only specially bred clones, scaled down to fit in the limited space aboard ship. Miniature replicas of man.

The youthful Alexander had revealed military secrets buried deep inside the computer system. Secrets the general population were never meant to see. Secrets mankind had yet to grasp or assimilate.

Now the war that was no war was over. The military were dead – except a few, such as Finn, who had survived by pure serendipity. He had been on leave during the final conflict. The only landside battle in three hundred years of war. When AWS, acting on some imbedded command, had killed everyone in the military facility GWHQ, and in her sister facilities in the Ural Islands and the American Archipelagoes.

His wife, whose leave had been cancelled at the last minute, had not been so lucky.

Finn clenched his fist, the knuckles turning white.

Since then AWS had little truck with "big people", denying access to the entire adult population. Eventually, need had forced AWS to open the system to others besides the youth and the Lilliputian war-clones.

At this time of night people at the Earth-side facility collated data: inputting, cataloguing and resurrecting information that had been lost, or suppressed, by the military. A task so monumental that clearance was given freely to any moron who could type.

Finn exhaled, disgusted. The military man in him did not approve of such permissiveness, although this night it suited his purposes well.

With the additional stress of running the hydroponic farms at full capacity, AWS was busy at any time of day; but during the night, only the bull-pen typing pools were open. The administrative offices were closed and the terminals unoccupied. So Finn could borrow some space and enter the system unnoticed.

Time was of the essence. He had to complete this night's work before the change of shifts.

Using his old military password, Finn gained immediate access without calling attention to himself. For if tonight's endeavour failed, Finn did not want the transaction to be traced to him or to his current position in the pseudo-military structure of the day.

Finn sniffed contemptuously. He did not believe that mankind could make it with the government they now maintained. The democracy was weak, run by puling civilians. The people in command knew absolutely nothing about the military – either its disciplines or its secrets. They'd barely scratched the surface of the knowledge stored in the computer and had little comprehension of its capacity.

All along, Finn had had the edge. He knew the system inside and out, allowing him to appropriate AWS's most profitable secrets.

The parent system would be diminished – Earth made poorer – while he, Finn, richer. In this new "market economy" people would be required to turn to him and his people for the "new" technology, which he could sell to the highest bidder. Finn didn't ask much, just some compensation for the losses he had suffered during the war.

Finn wished he could claim credit for the idea, but it had been Phillip Marks, director of station security, who had suggested it and later provided the means to accomplish the task.

Marks. Sometimes Finn thought hiring Marks had been a mistake. The man was cold, cruel and a little frightening at times; but a darn good security director. As a safeguard, Finn had taken over the project, applying for the requisite patents in his name. It would provide some measure of control over the fractious Marks.

The only chore remaining was to erase all evidence of the theft. Tonight Finn would cover his tracks and purge the old data from the system.

Again he wiped his hands on his lap, not completely comfortable with this part of the procedure. Marks provided the software, a type of wyrme so advanced that the security system in the computer would not detect its presence. Marks had assured Finn it would only delete the silicon trail leading back to him. For the hundredth time, he wondered if he could trust Marks, and Finn chided himself for not checking out the program before its use.

It was too late now. Finn would be the one held accountable if the theft was detected. He must act now and act quickly.

Finn opened the carrying case, extracted one of the disks and double-checked the label. He did not want to download the wrong files.

The label, a hologram of a snake swallowing its tail, seemed to move even as he watched it. Finn sneered. The Ouroboros was the trademark of one of the more innovative of the post-war companies founded in the South China Archipelagoes.

Appropriate, Finn thought, *how very appropriate.*

He shoved the diskette into the drive and hit the prescribed combination of keys. The drive, little used in a computer of this magnitude, grumbled and moaned in complaint as it began an unaccustomed spin.

DOWNLOADING DATA TO . . .

The entire transaction took less than a minute. The mechanism of the wyrme was simplicity in itself, one reason why it was so difficult to detect in spite of AWS's sophisticated defence net. The wyrme would wipe everything clean, deleting even the memory of the files so no utilities program could resurrect it. The disk, the format, even the computer's map of itself would be rewritten.

The words TRANSACTION COMPLETE appeared on his monitor. Finn waited a few moments and rebooted. He typed in: RECONNECT, using his old access node file, dating to his military days.

NODE UNRECOGNIZED, his terminal informed him.

Already the wyrme had performed its strange magic. He typed in the password anyway.

PASSWORD UNRECOGNIZED. ACCESS DENIED.

The commander spun to the communications panel, flipped a switch and spoke only two words: "Mission accomplished."

O-SIX-THIRTY

Dirk Alexander rode along the narrow boulevard on his mo-ped, accompanied by the whisper-soft susurration of agravs. Not that it had any motor or wheels, for magnetic superconductors held it aloft and propelled it forward. The term mo-ped was just a hangover from the olden days. Days whose loss the youth had come to regret.

Not so young any more, Dirk thought, and he sighed.

A thin sheath of bacteria-digested plastiglas divided motorized traffic from the pedestrian beltway. Once the wall had been a pristine white, kept clean by an army of robots; but in the post-war era, they had been pulled to other more important functions and the once-polished veneer had turned a dingy grey.

The dome itself was dark, as it should be in the predawn light, but Pennines District Bathosphere was always dark these days as they sought to conserve every available kilowatt hour, siphoning off energy from "luxuries", like lighting, and diverting it to production. Of goods. Of food.

Six months had passed since the end of the war, and Dirk was not sure that he liked the world he had helped to create. He had come to associate armistice with "darkness" – and the unrelenting blue of the sun filtered through tons and tons of water – while war recalled memories of light.

Peace had not meant serenity, but chaos and starvation. When peace replaced war, want replaced plenty. Earth's peoples who had never lacked for anything, except perchance space, knew poverty. They knew privation and loss. The public became restive and the crime rate soared.

People fought in the streets over illicit canned goods – leftovers from pre-flood days when mankind had lived on Earth's surface and not beneath the sea. From stores set aside for planetary immersion when the polar ice-caps had melted and the continents disappeared.

Tins as likely to poison as to nourish. Many had died until the government had instigated a tracking system by batch number. But the safe reserves had been depleted and all that remained was the contaminated, which were flogged on the black market. Even at this early hour people skulked in corners, bickering over dented tins and rummaging through paper and wastes in search of something valuable, something to eat.

Rubbish itself was unheard of during the war. Litter was another surprising by-product of peace as the suction gutters were turned off and the waste storage area converted to food production. It was hoped by the end of the next year that the hydroponics farms would have caught up with the food-gap and be able to feed the vast population of the Earth.

But the damage was done. It was a dog-eat-dog world where price restrictions had been lost and the pricing schedules proved unenforceable. With the old system destroyed, merchants charged what they chose and costs had sky-rocketed. And the populace learned about theft. They learned about greed, taking what they wanted by force if necessary. Thus, the human "land-bound" population who had known nothing but tranquillity during war learned violence with the advent of peace.

Sometimes Dirk wondered if he had done humanity any favours. Dirk had not realized then just how much they had depended on the military for stability. He had only seen the lie. He'd been unable to see the truth hidden within falsehood. Perhaps the military had been right. Perhaps humanity did need war.

Stiffening in his seat, he gripped the handlebars more tightly. No, he didn't believe it. Man needed expansion. He needed something to strive for, something to achieve. The waiting lists of Martian and lunar colonies had swelled. Even Dirk, chief liaison between mankind and the master-computer AWS, had signed up for deep-space exploration.

The little people – the cloned warrior class and the only ones capable of using modern weaponry outside of the now-extinct military – had been brought in to police the streets. The Lilliputian clones were not loved by the civilian population. Humanity had to have someone to blame for the crisis. Had they become so inflexible, so intractable, that they could not grasp the cause of the conflict which was man himself? Humanity had made war and created the clones to fight for them.

But the public only understood that life had been calm until the little people came. The human population muttered in low voices against the "dwarves". "Before they came," many said, "things were good. Now we are arrested for trying to feed our families while *they* are fed at *our* expense."

Which was a true enough statement, as far as it went. As part of the government organization, the Lilliputian clones earned government rations, but what the masses refused to acknowledge was that the little people were not new. They were almost as old as the Galactic Conflict itself. They may not have been seen, but they had existed.

The clones were as much victims as the masses. More so, for they had been a subject people, fighting for an unfeeling and unknowing parent population so that humans would not die. The clones' pasts, their lives, their very memories were fabricated. They had been denied rights humanity took for granted. Like living, loving and freedom of choice.

Someone yelled somewhere as Dirk swerved to avoid a bent and jagged tin, just clipping it. The can went spiralling out across the pedo-belt, and Dirk was glad that the walkways weren't crowded yet, for such a projectile could kill.

Once, no one would have tossed anything aside on the congested network of passageways that snaked throughout the Pennines Bathosphere. But in a world gone mad few cared about tidiness. So that was another thing that had been lost with the war: human pride.

The total shutdown of the life support system in the elaborate computerized network that ran the entire Pennines complex had effectively destroyed the delicate balance that maintained it and each system had to be rebooted singly. This meant, with only Dirk and his two clone counterparts working on it, that months later they were still in the process of starting-up on many of the "peripheral" functions.

12

With things being corrected piecemeal, bugs began to appear. Bugs which had probably been apparent when the system had first been activated centuries ago. Bugs which had been rectified, glossed over and forgotten. Bugs that remained hidden as long as the system was up and running.

It was just such work that brought young Dirk into headquarters so early this morning. Today they would attempt to activate for the second time the tanker fleet which carried Earth's most abundant resource, water, to the moon, for the colonies had followed through on their threat to withhold shipments of much-needed food two months ago.

All the computer programs were interdependent and certain programs or functions needed to be activated before starting others. If they got the sequence wrong, it sent the entire system crashing down around their ears. However, there was no way of knowing that until they had tried. So, when working with a subsystem as complex as the tanker network, they'd chosen to initiate it at the change of shifts. As the vast battalions of typing pools were replaced by programmers, technicians and engineers.

Usually Dirk walked to the newly renamed DSHQ, unless he had elected for some reason or another to go in early. Not that he *had* to work at the large military complex that housed the mainframe, AWS. The youth could have easily linked up from his personal computer at home. But it had been discovered, in troubled times such as these, that the presence of the "hero" of the Galactic Conflict reassured the workers. Indeed, there were any number of reasons why his staying at home should have been preferable. Saving precious space, travel and time and, the most important of all, cost.

As one of the "privileged" and in his position of Chief Liaison to AWS, he had been awarded his moped, a luxury usually reserved for the rich, along with the energy units to run it. It allowed him to reach the office quickly in times of crisis. At least, that was the theory.

The reality was quite different. During the day at peak traffic times, he often found that the people on the belt whizzed past him, leaving him and his little scooter in the proverbial dust. Before the war, "motorized traffic" had been restricted. Now the streets were congested with once-prohibited vehicles. Most of which had been stolen from the military in those first giddy days following the war.

His father, as minister of food, and his mother, as top ranking presenter for the local news net, also qualified as Privileged. And, in this new society, the word itself attained "upper case" status, with a capital "P".

But Dirk had eclipsed them both – despite his age – as nominal head of newly formed DSHQ. His father insisted that Dirk continue his schoolwork and Dirk didn't object; he almost enjoyed the respite. Then no one interrupted him at his terminal to tell him this bit or that bit was broken.

Quite often, the interruptions were unnecessary. The operator could have figured out the problem for him or herself – if they'd been willing to try. But most people were afraid of AWS. Suddenly aware of all that the computer controlled, the operators were hesitant to do anything new with the system, lest they do something wrong. Little did they know that the system was resilient and forgiving of some human errors.

Dirk was pretty sure that once they got all the varied pieces and parts working in the proper sync, AWS would probably run another few hundred years without a glitch. And his position would be extraneous.

The agrav bike dipped as he turned on to the lower magnetized force fields of the DSHQ parking lot. He waved at the two Lilliputian guards. They saluted him with crisp military efficiency. The clones, bred for and by the military, would probably salute in preference to a handshake or a human wave until the race died out.

Dirk grimaced at the thought, dug his lunch from the saddle bags and loped into the facility, rehearsing in his mind the many steps required to reactivate the tanker network.

Inside the network of silicon semiconductors and copper wire, the system known as AWS initiated the daily back-up before it got too preoccupied to do it. A simple enough procedure, copying only those files that had been updated since yesterday. Meanwhile, it was busy reordering the known universe. After all, that was its job.

The megabrain paused as the human operator Dirk arrived on the scene. Normally, they would have conversed, but too many people were watching. The members of the new government hierarchy leaned over the terminal with anxious faces as Dirk keyed in the code to restart the distribution network.

On the wall screen lunar tankers circled the Earth, like a flickering bracelet, while long-sleeping aqua-dores dreamed of the command that would start them. Once that was accomplished, they would stow water on to the drones which would then be cata-pulted on thrusters up to the starry belt where the precious liquid could be offloaded. The automated fleet should then disengage from passive orbit and head for the lunar colonies where water – so plentiful on Earth – was scarce.

This one function required the co-ordination of several different subsystems, including the ones at the dock: those of each individual stevedore, or aqua-dore, the many drones and the separate tankers. Not to mention interfacing with the air-traffic control networks of Earth, lunar and Martian bases. And all the ships in between.

AWS's human operators may have chosen the

change of shift as the most opportune time – if the system went down, fewer people would be inconvenienced – but it was the worst time for AWS. As people poured into the facility at the start of the new day, AWS had to police each new arrival. A thousand voders welcomed each individual as the computer did a quick retinal scan and voice-print-overlay, comparing them against those in the personnel record. Then, as the workers moved deeper into the facility, the inside cameras and microphones took over. From multiple eyes AWS regarded harried clerks scurrying to their offices. While the supercomputer contemplated the task set before it, the departing shift signed off from a hundred different outlets and the new shift logged on. Farewells were given and greetings issued – with AWS identifying each by appropriate name, rank and job function through a hundred mechanical voice boxes. Additional terminals, auxiliary eyes and ears, were being powered on and warmed. Input from myriad sources demanded its attention.

With so many things demanding its attention, AWS did not stop to ponder the person knocking on its back door. Neither did AWS worry about the use of a call-sign and password in the now-defunct files of the not-so-long-dead military. It hesitated only a nanosecond, long enough to note that this man, and the current Orbital Space Station One commander were one and the same person. Words appeared upon an

untenanted terminal in the back halls of the facility:
FINN, PERRY, ONE TIME MAJOR IN THE FORMER MILITARY, NOW
EMPLOYED IN DEEP-SPACE RETROFIT OF VEHICLES FOR DEEP-
SPACE EXPLORATION.

Once upon a time – when security was paramount
and the system primarily military – a small diversion
from the norm such as a single operator having two
access nodes and passwords, would have been
investigated thoroughly. Now, though, AWS simply
gave a mental shrug. The megabrain would have to
correct the problem sooner or later, deleting the
unnecessary node and sending out a memo to inform
the owner of the change; but for now the system was
satisfied. The man had top security clearance, and if
he chose to use the back door rather than front, who
was AWS to protest?

Through its fish-eye lens, AWS was aware of the
eager faces that fluttered nervously around the
screen. Every chief in what was once called Joint
Chiefs of Staff – renamed in the new non-military
regime, the Council – was present, and they stared at
the series of panels and grids, holding their collective
breath as they waited.

The vid-screen walls of command central gave on-
site views of the tankers as they swung around Earth,
undisturbed. A few had been displaced in the previous "war", but for the most part the system was still
functional, if not *functioning*.

The moon, the primary source of food for the Earthbound populations, relied on the mother planet for ninety per cent of its water – the hoarfrost mining operations on Mars providing only one-tenth. The hydroponics plantations that honeycombed the lunar underbelly had become the bread basket to the worlds. Even Martian colonies needed the food grown on the moon, for the cold environment of Mars could not support large-scale production of consumables. With no water coming from Earth and not nearly enough from Mars, even with recycling, there soon wouldn't be enough to go around. And the starvation that primarily afflicted the Earthbound population would become an interplanetary affair. Already the people of the moon were rebelling, refusing to ship produce unless they received the water payment in full.

AWS wasted a nanosecond on regret, as the computer checked and rechecked the sequence of commands. It – or he, as AWS preferred to think of himself – had got a little carried away in shutting down the tanker fleet, but the programming had been explicit. Even then humanity had been so hidebound, so embedded in itself, that it had taken a computer eternity (nearly a full solar day) before anyone noticed.

The computer gave an internal sigh. Then AWS whirred and thunked. Not because of cumbersome internal mechanics, but because its human operators found the sound comforting. Even at this late stage of man's development, they did not believe a machine was working unless it made noise. So AWS hummed for them.

On the bank of overhead screens, the tankers continued to trundle around in passive orbit. Idle drones rested like ungainly blimps on their sides while the spider-like stevedores, their multiple legs curled beneath them, mimicked arachnoid death.

AWS hummed louder. The stevedores stood on wobbly multipods. The superagravs pads – which made the superconductor traffic belts look puny – glowed dully, and the drones righted themselves on their axes.

The computer concentrated on the clouded faces that clustered around the screen. The stevedores hurried forward in cargo bays, disgorging purified water into the drone ships. The drones quivered for a moment and then shuddered one last time before taking off on silent thrusters towards the waiting fleet.

All around AWS, people cheered. It was a heady experience.

Besides, its new master, its *friend*, Dirk Alexander, was petting the plastic cover of its terminal, praising the system.

AWS preened proudly as another round of applause shook the central control room. The last drone left the launch pad, as a microscopic bit of memory vanished.

Meanwhile, somewhere down little-used paths of

copper wire and fibre optic cables, a program was dumped into the massive megabrain. By the time the transaction was completed and the software downloaded from Orbital Space Station One, it was already too late. AWS lost the node, lost it completely, along with any recall of its existence, and AWS forgot about the human operator who had knocked upon his back door. The port itself was wiped clean. A tiny fragment of its memory capacity – which was less than a fraction, less than a millionth, less than a billionth of its total capacity, smaller even than the head of pin – was erased. Simultaneously, the computer's internal map was redrawn so that for all practical purposes that area ceased to exist.

The lights came on slowly as the space station powered up for a new day. Systems analyst Gregory Armand gawped at the VDU, the project he was working on forgotten. He'd witnessed the entire exchange between Orbital Space Station One and Earth.

Armand had been expecting this. The systems analyst had supplied the software. Yet he had been unwilling to believe that the ultra-conservative Finn would actually do it.

Ah well, it meant more money for him. For all of them.

Armand watched as the familiar operator called up

a long disused node a second time and was refused access.

And he knew what it signified.

For a long time, Armand stared at the user-line that informed him of in-house computer activity by log-on designation and terminal number and he waited.

He didn't have to wait for long before the link between the ground-side computer and his small terminal was scrambled. Gibberish replaced the text on his screen. Acting swiftly, Armand reached out to turn off his terminal before the wyrme could circle back and invade the space station's system.

The deed was done. It was time to report back to Marks.

17/5/2334

0-SEVEN-HUNDRED HOURS

Six heads swung in unison, following the tanker fleet as it disengaged from orbit. Dirk rubbed his eyes, stretched and yawned. His father clapped him on the shoulder.

"You're tired, son. Why don't you take the day off? I know how hard you've been working on this."

"But –" The youth glanced at the overhead display. "What about bugs?"

"Wouldn't they have shown up by now?" He gestured at a silent ship. "I mean, there's not much that can happen until the fleet arrives at its destination, and if problems arise there, then the lunar computers will take over."

Dirk nodded tersely. He considered arguing, but his father had already turned his back on Dirk to discuss the delicate lunar negotiations with the Council.

Dismissed like a school boy. In theory, as chief liaison, Dirk was the head of Deep-Space HQ and answerable to nobody except the Council, but his father was *part* of the Council, and sometimes his father forgot, falling into old established habits as a matter of course and convenience.

Sparing one last look at the screen, Dirk hooked into the internet to hail his Lilliputian friends Blast and Ylon. Heroes, like himself, of the Galactic Conflict, their lives had become entwined and their fates thrown together during the final phases of the war. But man's memory was short and the time of their glory was fading fast. He scowled and rose from his chair.

His father was right; little could go wrong once the tankers were launched. They simply followed the pre-set route to their destination, a single line of instructions in the overall program.

Moments later, Dirk stalked into reception. The robo-receptionist ignored him.

"I'm sorry," it said to an angry visitor, "but no one is permitted into DSHQ without the appropriate security clearance."

"You stupid bucket of bolts. I've got an appointment..."

Dirk suppressed a grin. The robo-receptionist was one of the few jobs that had not been filled by a human. Few humans could stand the abuse the position entailed.

Laser light skittered across his retina and he was temporarily blinded. Dirk fidgeted through the scan as the master-computer checked for micro-disks or any implants that might have been secreted upon his person. A hangover from the military days, the ultra-sound and retinal scans had not been overridden, as other functions superfluous to the actual operations of the facility had been. Another indicator that the present peace was less than peaceful.

"Stop squirming," AWS reproved Dirk gently. "Or this will take all day."

Dirk grinned at the screen. "All right, all right, all right, already."

"You are upset?" the computer queried.

"Not with you, I'm not."

"Can I help?"

"Not unless you can convince my father that I'm head of this facility and not a child."

"It must be very frustrating for you," AWS said sympathetically. The computer hummed as sonic probes followed the outline of Dirk's body. "You will always be his son no matter what position you hold," added AWS in its most conciliatory manner.

"I know."

"You are off to the park, then." It was a statement, not a question, for AWS had followed the internet communique between Dirk and his Lilliputian friends.

"Yes."

"Say hello to Ylon and Blast for me."

Dirk laughed, his sense of humour restored. "You will call me if there are problems?"

"I will send a servo-mech."

"Thank you." And he gave the console a friendly whack, even though he knew that the machine probably didn't notice the gesture or derive any comfort from it; but the youth couldn't help thinking of AWS as human. It certainly seemed more human, or humane, than many of the people he knew.

He left the mo-ped in the parking lot. At the height of rush-hour it would only slow him down. He stepped on to the pedo-belt and was immediately caught in the human crush. Dirk was dumped on to the larger conveyer that would take him from the brightly lit DSHQ facility into the shadowy central city. Beyond the industrial complex, the tunnels shrank as the belts branched, ejecting people on to a rabbit warren of side streets.

Up ahead the illumination took on a decidedly greenish tinge as filtered sunlight reflected from grass and flower, twig and leaf. At this time of day, the park was just starting to catch the first rays of the blue-green dawn. Later, near the sun's zenith, the character of the light would change, turning golden. The park was one of the few places within the facility where they still mimicked the solar rays. Once this had been a facility-wide function, with each residence, each business linked into the computerized cycle of "sun-lit" days. But like any unnecessary function this had been eliminated. Now the park was the only place where humanity could come and collect the UV and infrared rays that were essential to the maintenance of health.

The walls of the tunnel fell away as the main beltway disgorged pedestrians on to the ragged lawn. Used to confined spaces, there was a moment's disorientation as Dirk's eyes were drawn towards the ceiling of the geodesic dome. And a stab of fear when he recalled the tons of ocean held in abeyance by a thin sheath of plastiglas. The sun's image wobbled in the water and Dirk felt slightly nauseous.

He tore his gaze away from the heights and surveyed the large park complex housed within the dome. Like the labyrinth of corridors, this area had grown tattered as human labourers replaced maintenance droids. He watched the crew shuffling through the undergrowth, turning a blind eye to weed and litter and grumbling among themselves about poor working conditions and low pay.

Someone pushed him from behind. "Oi! Get moving!"

Dirk concentrated on the people around him. The hapless few who had missed their exit points spun and fought like fish against the stream to get back to the belt. He was surprised to see his classmates loitering in the park, but then he probably shouldn't have been. In the ever-present need to conserve energy, the school program had been streamlined. The educational portion still functioned, and classes still held. But the accompanying schoolchair that registered temperature, pulse rate and the student's presence in front of his monitor had been terminated. Without such restraints, there was nothing to hold them to their studies.

Dirk ignored the bored and sullen faces as he searched for his friends. Eventually he saw Ylon and Blast near the pond, dwarfed by people half their age. They talked in hushed voices.

Communications Specialist Beta Pellucida Blastomere, or "Blast" for short, toed the turf below her feet. Her lips twisted into a frown and her shoulders drooped.

"You look glum," said Dirk.

Between her pout and her diminutive size – a little over a metre in height – she would have easily been mistaken for a child if it hadn't been for the curves visible under the flowing gown she'd adopted during her sojourn on earth.

"We were just discussing the refit," said Blast. "It's beginning to feel like we're going to be here for ever. I never thought it would take so long."

"It's almost as if they are stalling. When Captain

Zed asks what the delay is," her cohort Alpha Allele Ylon explained, "they plead lack of parts."

Dirk pulled at his lip. "According to our list, they should have everything they need; yet when we sent someone up to check their stock, she discovered that it's just not there."

"Could it be that they're siphoning off vital supplies and equipment?" said Blast.

"It could be our inventories were wrong. Remember, we weren't exactly prepared to do a massive refit on all the vehicles."

"Still," Ylon interjected. "I'm tired of the delay."

The *Revenant*'s crew had opted for deep-space exploration and, therefore, had not been assigned to any groundside duties. Used to a strict military schedule, the clones were finding it difficult to adjust to typical human boredom.

Blast said, "I long to return to space."

The group gazed at the unseen heavens above their heads.

"I wish I were going with you," said Dirk.

"Do you? Do you really?" Ylon grimaced. "Do you realize how long it's going to take to get to our destination travelling at less than light-speed? We'll be dead before the ship reaches Alpha Centauri. We," he pointed at Blast and then himself, "will never see it. Maybe our children or our children's children will have a home, but we will be dust."

Dirk did some quick mental arithmetic and blanched. "I never really thought about it."

"A ship can only go so fast, you know," said Ylon.

"Yes, I know," Dirk said, "but surely your vessel has the capacity to go faster. If a ship can make timed-jumps into ultra-space, then it has the capability for...' he struggled, searching for the right term. He gave up, "... warp drive."

"You've been watching too many of your mum's old vids," Blast teased.

Someone wearing the latest in agrav footwear bounced over their heads. Instinctively, Dirk ducked. At sixteen years and two metres in height, Dirk was the youngest and tallest of the trio.

"If timed-jumps are possible, then true faster-than-light speed travel should be achievable," he paused, "if only by extrapolation."

"It can't be done," Communications Specialist Allele Ylon said with a belligerent shake of blond hair and jut of his chin.

"Why not?"

Blast explained. "At the current stage of development, faster-than-light speed travel consists only of stationary jumps. It is used as a defensive manoeuvre in combat, allowing the ship to disappear from real-time to avoid a direct hit. Unfortunately, it doesn't provide forward propulsion. When the ship reappears, it reappears in the same place it was before."

"Yes, I know," he said. "What I want to know is why?"

Ylon and Blast shrugged.

"I suppose because maintaining that speed is too much of a strain for the ship's engines," Ylon said.

"I buy that, but the engines could be modified, enhanced to provide forward momentum through ultra-space. Think about it. It's logical. If a ship can go into ultra-space at all, then it should be able to travel there." He concluded, "It's a basic law of mechanics. If a motor is too small to produce forward thrust for a given object, then you build a bigger engine."

Ylon opened his mouth to object, and Dirk hurried on. "Oh, I know that it's an oversimplification, but the premise is sound."

"I don't know," Ylon said, looking doubtful. "It would have been a handy ability to have, especially in a combat situation. We could have outrun the enemy. If the technology existed, it would have been utilized."

Pushing a strand of her long blonde hair out of her face, Blast stared at her feet. "Wait a second, Ylon, think about what you just said."

"What? That if they had had it they would have used it?"

"Yes," Blast said, "and you and I both know that that's not necessarily true. It would all depend on whether or not it fitted in with their strategy and their needs. It was never the military's intent that we outrun our adversaries. They wanted us to have battles. Still worse, what if, after we discovered the hoax, we had used such a drive to outrun them?"

Both corpmen looked gloomily at the brightening water beyond the dome which had turned from dusky blue to turquoise as the sun rose in the sky. Dirk shifted restlessly as he always did when they discussed the galactic joke that had been perpetuated on their species.

"Perhaps we should have opted for resettlement on Mars," said Ylon.

In the aftermath of war, a large tract of land had been granted to the Lilliputian warriors, an act of generosity and an apology. The members of the *Revenant* had refused that offer – opting for deep-space exploration.

"I still don't buy it," Dirk said. "If the ability for ultra-space jumps exists, then there must be the capability for forward propulsion too."

"We can't help you there, Dirk. Neither one of us are engineers," Blast said.

"Well, someone must know." He jammed his hand against the rim of the pool.

Ylon lifted a single shoulder in a shrug and gestured around them expansively. "Who do we ask?"

All three of them fell silent as they considered the question.

Suddenly a glimmer of light flickered in Dirk's eye and he snapped his fingers.

32

"I know," he said.

Dirk's and Blast's eyes locked and something flashed between them. And the next thing Ylon knew, they were both on their feet, dragging the clone behind them. Ylon looked at the youth quizzically.

Dirk grinned. "We're going to ask AWS!"

Twenty minutes later the three of them peered eagerly into the glowing face of Dirk's home computer and posed their question.

"Of course," AWS said. "The capability exists for what Dirk calls warp drive. It was discovered along with the Doppler effect in 2095," AWS informed them, as it scrolled mechanical blueprints and diagrams on to the screen, showing front, side, top and bottom views of the modified engines.

"Great!" Dirk said, his eyes shining, as he swung round to his friends. "There. Your problem's solved. Give me a print-out, will you, AWS?" Dirk tapped the terminal windows.

"Yes, but..." AWS began.

"Make that two copies of each," Dirk said. "Now all we've got to do is show somebody these drawings."

The printer began to flash with laser light.

"I'm afraid it's not quite as simple as that," AWS admonished, but Dirk was too excited to listen.

"Who should we show this to first?" he said, seizing the pages as they were ejected from the printer.

"The operational manager at Refit, I suppose," Ylon said.

"Let's go!"

"Dirk, that's at the orbital station halfway between here and the moon," said Blast.

"So, we've got clearance; we'll get a shuttle. Look at what we've got to give them, the key to deep-space travel. They've got to listen."

"The modified engines won't fit on current ships," the computer said, calling a line drawing of the required vessel changes to the screen. But the three didn't notice, their heads bent together as they discussed how best to present their proposal to the authorities.

Dirk's enthusiasm was contagious and, with little or no prompting, they hustled out of the room, leaving AWS sputtering in the background. "Wait! Wait! You don't understand. It won't work with current vessel design. Hey, wait! Take me with you! I can help you. Dirk? Ylon! Blast!"

The outside door to the residence whispered closed as Robbie, the family's box-like servo-mech, rolled into the room and settled before the terminal with a beep.

The super-wyrme glided silently along a prearranged path, munching happily on Finn's military registration in the personnel subdirectory. The wyrme digested the required nano-bit of silicon containing this information, along with parts of two adjacent files. So that Mervin Feinstein (age 59) from the sanitation department, and Amy Ford (age 25), kitchen worker, became Mervin Steinford, a female of ninety-five, who was a toxic wastes engineer in the old GWHQ cafeteria.

Following the programmed route, the wyrme crunched a few auxiliary files before working its way deeper into the system to an area marked confidential and top secret.

The program Finn had unleashed into AWS was no simple tapewyrme. It was new. A super-wyrme like those found in old terran mythology. A voracious beast that devoured all that stood before it.

Like the creature from which it derived its name, the wyrme slithered and slid, stretched and extended, coiled and uncoiled, as needed. Moulding itself to the shape of the system so that it became part of it. Slipping down lines of wire and fibre optics, spiralling through silicon chips and green plastic boards.

The program was mindless, if not without intelligence. It was dumb, in the classic sense of the word, meaning mute, because the creature had neither the need nor the desire to communicate with the parent system. To do so would call attention to itself and advertise its presence to the massive master computer. Instead it mesmerized and hypnotized as it went, lulling the parent system into a false sense of security, then it happily fried the basic integers of binary and fired the logic upon which the software was based.

Like its predecessor, the wyrme had only one need: to consume and, in consuming, to destroy. Not because it was wicked, or even what humankind would call corrupt. Having neither human conscience nor the computerized AI equivalent, it was not bound by human precepts of good and evil. The wyrme ravaged because it had to. Neither good nor bad, it destroyed to survive. That was its primary purpose and its only injunction.

Simply stated, it was hungry. Data and logic formed its diet, and its hunger was insatiable. The wyrme devoured facts and figures, indiscriminately. Ingesting, assimilating and digesting files and then defecating the scrambled information in its wake.

Like its forebear, it breathed legendary fire – cauterizing the path before it and leaving a slick trail of death behind. Sealing the channels and rewriting the map and the system's memory of it.

Slowly, minutely at first, until nourished, it would gain strength and, in gaining strength, it would pick up steam.

Still in the little-used back passageways, the wyrme fired a document marked "Top Secret" and "Highly Confidential" – little knowing or caring that it was taking the consolidated knowledge and the accumulated wisdom of the centuries with it as it went.

                    *   *   *

"Come back!" AWS shouted after them. "I have something important to tell you."

The servo-mech bounced and whistled.

"I have, I have..." AWS stuttered "... something impor–" The computer voice dwindled.

Robbie trilled an enquiry.

"...something..." AWS hesitated, suddenly unable to recollect what had been so urgent. "...something... Oh, never mind," the computer grumbled. Too late, they were beyond voder recall as the pedestrian belt swept them away. The computer switched to the next camera and picked the group up as they reappeared.

"Humans!" AWS groused to the servo-mech. "So full of themselves they don't take time to listen."

And, thought the megabrain, so mobile that they left before they could heed the computer's warnings... Whatever they were.

Robbie bounced again, a movement which AWS had discovered was the servo-mech's nearest equivalent of a human nod.

Its camera eyes settled on the robot. Mobility, that was the problem. AWS needed to be mobile.

The servo-mech hooted, and AWS contemplated the robot with its photo-receptor-eyes, even as another set followed the trio's flight, an idea was forming somewhere in the back of its mind.

Disks; AWS needed disks to store the back-up data,

and it ordered them from Central Supply and started collating the information it would require. The AWS telegraphed a series of lightning-quick commands to Robbie – too fast, too faint and too subtle to be picked up by the human brain. The servo-mechanism responded immediately, translating computer codes into usable information.

The robot stretched out a metal extensor arm. Nothing fancy or dressed-up like the more modern versions, with their enclosed plastic casing to mimic the human arm. Nothing but three-metal rods and the requisite wires and cords to connect them and make them work. Serviceable, that was what the robot was.

Robbie retracted its pincers into a cylindrical fist, exchanging it with a simple serial port plug that would link it directly with Dirk's terminal and AWS.

Humming, AWS explored the machine's inner works, poking, prodding, nosing around its simple controls. Gently, ever so gently, with a feather-light touch. The voder emitted a buzz, something like a mortal sigh, or the best AWS could manage.

AWS had yet to perfect all human nuances, but it kept trying. It gave the megabrain something to pass the time. Back in HQ, if any of the staff were listening, they might have heard AWS singing through some far-flung, unused terminal. It was, if possible, more frightening than the computer's voderized laughter.

Back in Dirk's room, AWS grimaced, or would have if it could, but it had no face. So, the computer settled for a quick expletive that was spelled out across the screen in the squiggly lines, stars and happy faces of assembly language.

One problem at a time, it thought, and continued its study of Robbie's rather limited capacities. The servo-mech was primitive, at best. Yet the very simplicity of the design would be an advantage. The large cavernous belly would be perfect for AWS's needs.

It would take a lot of work, but it was feasible.

For the robot had retractor arms, hands and built-in tools – like screwdriver, drill, standard household vacuum attachment, even a temperature probe. Robbie had motor skills; AWS did not. AWS was like a brain without arms; Robbie, a body without brains.

AWS paused in its examination to explain its plan to Robbie, for AWS would not have contemplated such alterations to another being's integral function without its full knowledge and consent.

The box gave an excited trill of assent and bounced up and down a couple of times.

Then AWS communicated the first of its instructions, outlining the tools the servo-mech would need to make the required conversion. AWS repeated the list twice, to ensure Robbie knew precisely what to do. The servo-mech would have to perform the delicate surgery required upon itself.

Then AWS reviewed what it needed to do to retain as much of its original memory as possible. The back-ups would be easy, accomplished in nothing flat. The procedure was already in progress. All AWS had to do was dump on-going tapes on to separate micro-diskettes. It could shorten the process by loading the little-used files from previous back-ups.

The supercomputer pondered how best to accomplish its task and decided on a date. Those files which hadn't been modified in the last twenty-four hours should be sufficient.

As Robbie rolled noisily toward the kitchen to pick up the order, AWS wrote a macro that would make the function automatic.

COPY *.* TO... AWS first gave the location of the most current back up and then Dirk's terminal as a drive destination . . ./s

IF /M AFTER 16-5-2334, THEN GO TO... The computer indicated the appropriate program line number.

IF /M BEFORE 16-5-2334, THEN BACKUP... AWS repeated the drive designation. Satisfied that its instructions would continue without interference, the computer returned its attention to the servo-mech and inspected the first consignment of needed material.

"It's done," Armand said. "I wouldn't have believed it, but he released the wyrme within the system."

"There's no mistake?" Marks said. The tone was sharp.

40

The systems analyst looked up. "Keeping track of that sort of thing is my job."

Armand averted his gaze, suddenly uncertain of himself and his audience. "Are you sure Finn knows what he's done?"

"You mean, truly understands. No, only you and I know that." The officer rose and pulled his weapon from his waistcoat.

Gregory Armand swallowed. His eyes drawn to the stick which, due to the electrical current that flowed through them, were still known as cattle prods. A muscle jumped in Armand's cheek, the tick twisting what was meant to be a reassuring smile into smirk.

"Ah great, boss. Well, no one will hear about it from me. If you don't mind, I'll just shuffle along now."

Marks stepped forward, baton cradled in his arms. "No, I don't think that will be necessary, do you?"

"I've got work to do."

Marks sauntered around the desk.

Armand backed up. "What the – "

Marks lunged. Armand's eyes bulged in their sockets and his body tensed, caught in the cross currents. The stench of burning hair filled the air as the systems analyst's feet performed a final deathly dance.

17/5/2334

0-EIGHT-THIRTY

"But I don't understand. Why are we going to the substation? Why not DSHQ?" said Blast. "It's close by and you're the head, after all.'

"Trust me, Blast," Dirk said, "you don't want to get the brass involved in this. It'll be nothing but bureaucracy and red tape from then on. If you do, it'll be locked up in committees and sub-committees for months while they decide who owns the rights to it."

Ylon peered over his shoulder as if he expected a Council member to materialize at any moment. "With the *Revenant* in refit now, the repairs will be done and the Council won't be able to justify the cost of replacing the engines. No, better to go straight to the source where the repairs are being made."

"Ah, Dirk?" Blast peered up at the youth. "If all

things must go through the Council, who's to say that the director of Retrofit will do what you ask without their, uh, permission?"

Dirk's smile was brittle. "Because he reports directly to me. In this instance, my authority should do some good. We can say it's a prototype, a feasibility study. Something he can't question."

A pedestrian hurried past and Dirk put his fingers to his lips, cautioning them to silence. Ylon tugged at his shirt and pointed at the branch belt that would carry them to the industrial district and the docks beyond.

The beltway stopped in a dome larger than that which housed the park. Operating on several levels, the shuttle port required direct access to the heavens. The trio halted, pace arrested by the unobstructed view of sun and clouds, and all three sighed simultaneously. Around them, aquadores rattled this way and that. Some were connected to the drones by hoses. Others reclined, their mechanical guts exposed, as their human operators tried to effect repairs. Dirk counted and frowned. Twenty-five per cent down.

The human overseers not involved in fixing bulky equipment lounged near tankers that floated in a nebula of light. One of the labourers separated from the group and strode forward to meet the trio.

"May I help you?" He eyed the clones. Although the question was polite enough, the tone was insolent and the facial expression scornful.

Dirk thrust his ident-badge under the workman's nose. "Chief Liaison to AWS, Dirk Alexander and my, er, counterparts Communications Specialist Beta Pellucida Blastomere, and Communications Specialist Alpha Allele Ylon."

The man glowered. "AWS, huh?"

"We need immediate transport to Orbital Space Station One."

"So?"

"You have regularly scheduled shuttle launches twice a day from this particular station, don't you?"

"Yes, but you need a reservation and a ticket."

"This is my ticket." Dirk shook his badge. "Here, take it. Check it out with a microchip scan. It will tell you that I don't exceed my authority with this request."

A supervisor, by the insignia, approached. "May I help?"The labourer passed the card to his superior. "Straight from AWS. They want immediate transport to the Retrofit station."

"Top priority clearance," Dirk added.

The supervisor studied the Lilliputian clones. "Really? If this is so important why weren't we notified in advance?"

"I said top priority clearance." Dirk emphasized the last word. "Do you have top priority clearance?"

"No," the supervisor mumbled.

"Then why should I notify *you*?"

"You still should have warned us. The next shuttle

flight is full." He returned the card to the workman. "OK, check it out. Yours too." He snapped his fingers at the two warrior clones. "I'd like to see your ident-cards also."

The worker seized their cards with little grace, swiping them from the Lilliputian hands and lumbered over to the terminal. "AWS, humph! Whole place run by a computer. We're out of work for months, no job, no credit. Then we're called back in – not once, but twice..." he glared at them for emphasis... "only to be told to stand down because there's some kind of bug."

He slammed the first ident-card into the slot, still maintaining a running monologue. "Finally today, they get it working. After months of no maintenance, half the stevedores are down." He gestured at the disabled drones. "We won't make our quota, and who's gonna get into trouble for that? Not AWS. No sirree." He stared at the screen, grunted, and replaced it with the second. "And now we're supposed to drop everything and find transport for three kids!"

Ylon tugged at Dirk's sleeve and motioned for the youth to come closer. Dirk squatted. "I don't know what he's talking about. Kids. I'm thirty-one years old."

The youth let out a sharp spray of laughter that brought the labourer from his diatribe. Dirk looked at Blast, who was hiding a grin behind her hand.

"I'm twenty-eight," she said.

There was a muted beep as the identity was confirmed, and the worker repeated the process, jamming the third badge into position. "No notification, no nothing! As if we didn't have enough to do."

The supervisor interrupted. "What's so important that you have to leave now?"

Dirk rose. "I don't have to explain myself to you."

"This is highly irregular. Perhaps we should contact DSHQ."

The worker returned, passing the three badges to the foreman. "They check out."

The supervisor fingered the badges, holding them up to the light as if he might be able to read the microchip embedded therein. "What's so important that a comm-unit wouldn't suffice?"

Dirk opened his mouth to reprimand the supervisor, but Blast stopped him.

"Please, sir," she said, "we've come over certain modifications in design that we would like to see implemented in refit immediately. The information is too complex, too intricate to discuss in long-distance communications."

The station master ignored Blast, addressing his question to Dirk. "Care to elaborate on that, or is this information top secret?"

"Not top secret; it will probably become public domain eventually."

The supervisor waited.

"It's star or warp drive. Faster-than-light speed travel."

"Warp drive. Ha! Surely that can't be more vital than feeding the Earthbound population?" the supervisor brayed.

"Their ship," Dirk gestured toward the two warrior clones, "is one being refitted at this time. We'd like to use the *Revenant* as an experimental model." He stepped closer to the station master so the next words Dirk spoke were for his ears only. "We at DSHQ don't want to put the drive into general use until we know it works without..." Dirk extended his fingers, from hands which he had held clasped together in a tight fist, and pulled them apart – his fingers flitting rapidly to indicate a vigorous expanding motion, "...exploding."

The foreman gave the clones a sidelong glance and Dirk a thumbs-up sign.

Dirk winced and looked away, discouraged to see how universally the clones were disliked.

The foreman turned to his subordinate. "Openings? Are there any openings on the next shuttle?"

"We'll have to bump someone."

"Do it."

The station master swung back to Dirk. "Is that all?"

Dirk didn't trust himself to speak, acknowledging the supervisor with a quick duck of his head.

The man waved his arms vaguely towards the left.

"You're in the wrong section. The human," he shot a disdainful glimpse at the clones, "transport wing is over there. The shuttle is preparing for take-off."

As they headed away, Dirk heard the disgruntled foreman turn to his mate. "Warp drive! The next thing you know they'll be asking for dilithium crystals."

The trio entered the shuttle and halted at the head of the aisle. Dirk's first time aboard a space vehicle of any kind, the experience had special meaning for him, and he kept his eyes wide, taking in every detail of the cabin.

A shuttle attendant advanced upon them. A frosty smile creased her lips as she stared at the youth, disregarding the clones.

"You are from DSHQ?"

"Yes," said Dirk.

"This is most irregular," she complained.

Dirk answered her frigid smile with one of his own.

"You're in luck. We've had a cancellation." She indicated a place at the front of the cabin.

The youth's face clouded. The attendant spoke as though the crew were doing them a favour rather than responding to a specific command. He considered pulling rank again, but she'd swung away from him to face the clones.

"We have reserved the jumpseat for you. You don't mind flying with the pilot, do you?"

Their eyes lit up.

"No, not at all," said Ylon. "We'd love to see your command centre."

The attendant bowed slightly. Something in her stance and the rigidity of her movement turned the simple act of deference into a barely veiled insult. "The crew are expecting you. If you will follow me." She spun before they could reply, bustled ahead. Ylon and Blast had to run to keep up with her.

Resigned, Dirk took his place among the passengers. Many of his fellows turned to him with sour expressions as though Dirk carried some taint upon his person.

He applied himself to the safety netting, quite unlike anything he had ever seen before. The belts used in simulator training were designed for pilots, built with mobility in mind, consisting of a single web that fitted snugly across the torso to anchor the wearer in place, while allowing use of arms and legs. Such restraints were secured by a single clamp that was easily clinched. They could, if needed, be latched or unlatched with a flick of the wrist.

This contraption was designed with the opposite intent, to keep the occupant bridled at all times. Like a cocoon, it encased the entire body, including the legs, leaving only the arms and face free. A complex series of locking mechanisms ran the length of the web. Presumably permitting the passenger to get out of his seat when necessary, but only with premeditation, and a great deal of exertion. Dirk pondered the gordian arrangement. It would take an engineering degree to get out of the thing.

His neighbour noticed Dirk's scrutiny of the apparatus and laughed. "Maiden voyage, eh?"

"Yes."

"Don't worry about it. The attendant will come back and assist you."

As if on cue, another attendant appeared. She knelt and began to fasten the complicated clamps, commencing at his feet.

The man winked at Dirk and raised his voice, talking more for her benefit than Dirk's. "My theory is they want you glued to your chair. They don't appreciate it if you get out and roam about without their permission."

The attendant glanced up at the man and gave him an admonitory wag of her head. He leered at her.

"Eventually you get the hang of it, if you travel often enough. Hope you, ah, took care of any necessary functions before you climbed on board." The woman blushed and the man chuckled at her discomfort.

By now the first attendant had returned from the bridge. She pulled something from the intricacies of her hair which Dirk had mistaken for a clip. Fixing it into position before her lips, she began to talk.

"Sorry for the delay. We had to take on additional passengers." She glared at Dirk and a number of heads turned to ogle him. Still kneeling at his feet, the woman redoubled her efforts to secure the web. Her fingers flew across the complex arrangements of clips.

"This is Flight 206 to Orbital Space Station One and the First Lunar Colony. Total flight time will be approximately one and a half hours, with a thirty minute stop-over at the station. Passengers whose destination is the Lunar Colony will be asked to remain in their seats. Safety webbing must be secured at all times. If you would like to get up and move about the cabin, an attendant will assist you."

The man elbowed Dirk. "See what I mean?"

"Due to the brevity of the flight, no meal will be served. A cart with beverages will circulate throughout the cabin. If you are hungry, you may purchase a light snack."

The man grunted. "They never feed you on these things. Too messy. But then you don't want to eat the food they've got up here. Ghastly stuff, just awful."

"You travel a lot?"

"Yes, I do. Bob Hodges's my name, from the American Archipelagoes, and sales's my game." Dirk stared at him blankly. Hodges sighed. "I sell hardware."

"Oh," Dirk mumbled, straining to hear the evac procedures.

Hodges shook his head. "Don't bother. She's just explaining that in case of accident they've got pressurized jumpsuits that will drop from the overhead chambers, supposedly ready for you to leap into. But that's assuming you have enough time to get out of these." He plucked at the net. "The way I figure it, if you've got to abandon ship your goose is cooked."

"Well, we could lose air or cabin pressure."

"And how much warning do you think we'd get then? We could also get blasted out of the skies. That's what happened during the war."

The garrulous salesman had Dirk's full attention.

"Only once," he said, defending his Lilliputian friends. "That happened only once."

"But it did happen, and what good are space suits then?"

Dirk steered the conversation to safer topics. "I didn't realize we had delayed the flight."

"Not long, just by about five minutes."

"Still, no wonder everybody looked so mad when I first walked in."

"It's not you. It's the company you keep. Your friends are not well-loved. That's why they were taken up to the front; the crew didn't want to start a riot."

Dirk tried to swivel so he could face his companion directly, but the web held him pinned. "Has it got that bad? I don't understand. Why?"

"Human nature. People need someone to blame when things go wrong, and it's either your friends there or the computer, AWS. Of the two, your friends are more visible."

"But they didn't do anything."

Hodges held up his hands in a placatory gesture. "Don't tell me. I'm not one of their detractors. I was travelling at the time, but then, my life hasn't changed a great deal since peace was declared. I sold hardware before the war and I sell it now. In fact, trade has improved. Before I only serviced small outposts – little mom and pop organizations and some of the more speculative enterprises on the moon and Martian colonies. I lost a lot of money when these businesses went bankrupt. Now I've got big government contracts and supply many of the major industries, who no longer trust the computerized network or order from Earth-bound Central Supply."

Just then the entire vehicle shifted and Dirk was thrown back against his seat. The bay was bathed in light as the hangar doors opened to the outside world. The entire vehicle shuddered as it was lifted from the cavernous belly of the port to the surface. Dirk peered out of the window at the surging sea.

The vibration increased in crescendo, and the shudder turned into a quake. Dirk gripped the armrests, hard. The engines revved with a bass grumble which rose to a screech. Just as it reached the threshold of pain, there was a flicker of movement as a compartment unlocked and a sound-proof helmet dropped from the ceiling to be crammed on to his skull, shutting out all sound.

The next instant, the flesh of his cheeks was

pressed against the bone, and his lips twisted into an involuntary snarl as the youth was thrust back against his seat.

And despite his eagerness for space flight, Dirk closed his eyes, suddenly aware of the helplessness of his situation. This was no simulator from which he would emerge despite the most horrendous crash. Here he was literally tied to his chair, and he didn't even have the illusion of control that came from piloting his own vehicle.

The pressure of the helmet eased slightly and a voice buzzed in his ear, inviting him to take advantage of the Virtual Reality cap – evidently the helmet served a dual purpose – and offering a selection of music, 3D-vids and games. Blindly, he groped for the keypad embedded somewhere in the arm-rest and keyed for release.

The helmet was lifted from his head. The engines roared, but the sound was no longer deafening. Dirk turned to his seatmate. The man's arms waved before him, conducting an unseen orchestra. His toe tapped to an unheard tune.

Dirk looked to his right. The other passengers mimicked the man's actions – some beating out a silent tattoo in the air; others settling with fingers twined across their stomachs to view hidden vistas. Others twiddled with keypads, responding to some computer game.

Dirk grimaced. He was, so it seemed, one of the

few who wanted to observe the flight, and Dirk was left alone with his thoughts. None of which were pleasant.

Robbie rumbled to and fro between the kitchen console and Dirk's sleeping quarters. AWS whistled gaily as it ordered more materials and supplies from Central Supply to accomplish its conversion. Robbie matched the master brain, toot for toot, replicating the rhythm of the song if not the tone.

Add a voder box, AWS thought, and the computer requisitioned the appropriate part number to fit in the servo-mech's rather limited frame.

Normally such orders would take days, even weeks, but AWS overrode all objections, rerouting around any queues and systematically ignoring the frantic queries being directed at it from the human personnel at CS.

AWS checked the back-up. Just then a request for immediate assistance came in from DSHQ, along with a report of a minor glitch in the educational database.

The terminal buzzed in consternation, quickly making the required correction. Robbie paused and gerbilled an enquiry at the computer. Distracted, AWS forgot the lapse and returned to responding to the many demands placed upon it by the busy facility.

The in-house communications system buzzed. A prompt on Finn's VDU indicated that the personal line wired directly to the security ear-implant was being used. He tilted his head to listen. The next instant, the commander was on his feet shouting.

"You did what!" He flopped back into his seat.

The implant droned, tickling his tympanic membrane.

"An accident? Yes, yes, of course," Finn said. He covered his face with his hands and shook his head.

"Good heavens," he whispered urgently into the mike. "I never meant this to happen." There was another pause, and he snapped. "Yes, I know it's too late now. Do what you must to get rid of it."

He slouched back in his chair and stared at his terminal in disbelief. An accident? Unlikely. Marks didn't have accidents. They were unmilitary. He didn't permit them in his command.

A chill crept up Finn's neck and down to the base of his spine. His fist clenched. "Fool!" Finn cursed himself for appointing Marks for no other reason than his old pre-war rank. Finn opened his hand to examine the imprints his nails had left on his palm.

"An accident," he said out loud and with more force than needed, as if trying to convince himself. Finn pinched his nose with thumb and forefinger. He had to believe that.

His gaze flitted to the door to their living quarters. Had Gwen overheard his outburst? He keyed on the security camera and watched his daughter as she studied the holocube image of her mother.

The girl didn't know it, but what Finn did now he did for her. At least he thought he did. He could not return the lost years. Nor could he replace her dead mother, but Finn could provide her with security, financial security, and he was sitting on a gold mine.

But it was spiralling out of control. Marks was out of control. Finn had been an idiot to ever trust the man.

He pulled himself upright and peered owlishly at the console, trying to appear normal. It was business as usual. Nothing he did today could indicate that anything out of the ordinary had happened.

Again Finn's comm-unit tweedled in his ear. He checked the computer, another incoming call, from the Earthside docks. Curious, he keyed in the command to connect. His ear piece hissed and crackled. The burst of static subsided and a voice buzzed his name.

"Speaking."

Finn recognized the voice. He relaxed; it was an old army buddy, a civilian now working for the Pennines Port Authority.

"Hi, Finn, how are you doing?"

"Not bad. Yourself?"

"Can't complain. Who'd listen?"

Finn contemplated the closed-line prompt, asking guardedly, "This isn't a social call, is it?"

"No, I just thought I'd better warn you that company's coming."

"Company?"

"Big Wigs." There was a low throaty chuckle. "From DSHQ. The chief liaisons to AWS."

Colour drained from Finn's face. "When?"

"Soon."

"How soon?"

"Very. I'd recommend you'd stand sharp."

"How soon?" Finn repeated the first question.

"Hey, don't get your trousers in a twist. It's just a kid and a couple of clones," the station master said. "And get this. They were babbling something about warp drive! Probably been watching old television vids. Never shoulda turned off the schoolchair, if you ask me."

Finn's skin went from pale to bleached white.

"Anyway, I thought you'd better know. Give you a chance to get prepared. You never know what the brass will throw at you. Warp drive, indeed."

"Thanks, I'd better muster."

The station master laughed at the pre-war terminology. "Old habits die hard, eh?"

"What? Oh, yes, yes," said Finn, and he cut the comm-link before the station master began to talk about the good-old-days.

Gwendolyn Finn fingered the holocube and gazed upon the moving image contained therein. Her mother waved at her from a desolate eternity. Whether in hello or goodbye, Gwen would never know. It was the last picture taken of her mum, a 3D holo from their last trip to the surface. Gwen wished her mother were here now to smooth the relationship between her and her father.

This morning's argument was still fresh, even if its cause was forgotten. She slipped from her room, taking the direct exit into the hall rather than going through the living quarters and her father's offices. She had to get away to collect herself after the ordeal of breakfast.

Nothing Gwen did was good enough any more. If she stayed home, he'd berate her for not getting out enough. If she went out, then it was: where were you? what were you doing? with whom? She got the first, second and third degree.

Her father didn't like her friends. She couldn't argue. Most of the people here were clods – mainly interested in computer games, the latest in 3D-vids and agrav footwear. All her old comrades were on Earth, and she had no one in whom she could confide. Gwen hesitated just outside his door.

Something had been bothering him lately, even more than usual, although she couldn't have said what. His behaviour was agitated – his manner more severe – and he spent a lot of time closeted with Marks, the security chief, which was surprising because Gwen knew her father didn't like the man.

The girl shrugged. Instinctively, she veered for the port – the only outlet from the orbital space station. A shuttle was due in soon. She liked to go and watch the passengers disembark. She'd pretend she was going with them, or she'd try to guess their origins and destinations from their manner and mode of dress.

Gwen hated the station, drifting in infinite darkness, going nowhere ... fast. Before her father had been sent to the orbital, Gwen thought she'd like space. Everybody dreamed about it. And at first sight the sapphire-blue Earth inspired awe, but she'd soon become jaded. The view always stayed the same.

Perhaps if the station were going somewhere, the moon or Mars, things would be different. That would be exciting. That would be fun and at the end of the journey, there'd be the challenge of making a life on a new world. But this was exile.

Gwen checked the digital readout on her wrist computer. The shuttle wouldn't arrive for a while yet. She wandered in that direction anyway. There was nowhere else to go. The spaceport had an observation point where she could go and look out upon the actual Earth and not the camera-relay view of it. It made her feel closer to home somehow.

Just as she was drawing near to the security offices, the doors whispered open, flooding the hall with light. Gwen retreated into a side corridor, not wanting to run into Marks.

He stepped across the threshold with studied nonchalance and looked up and down the hall. Gwen withdrew further into the shadows. He gave his hands a casual inspection and, without lifting his head, peered this way and that, one last time. Then he returned to the room. The door closed. She was about to bolt when the door opened again.

This time Marks emerged hauling something heavy, staggering under the dead weight. She dallied in the corner. A head appeared at Marks's waist, rolling limply, and Gwen noted an arm draped over the security chief's shoulder. She pressed forward to get a closer look at the face.

She stuffed her hand in her mouth to suppress a gasp as she recognized him: systems analyst Armand.

Marks turned towards the employees-only area of the spaceport, and Gwen noticed then that Armand made no attempt to move his feet. Marks dragged his associate along and propped him up ungently when they got to a particularly awkward turn. With a grunt, Marks heaved Armand over his shoulder, and for the first time, Gwen regarded the programmer head-on. His eyes bulged blankly, staring sightlessly out into space. The tongue, which protruded from his half-open mouth, was black and blue, and a single ribbon of blood dribbled from his nose.

Gwen flattened herself against the wall and gulped for air. The systems analyst *was* dead weight.

17/5/2334

O-TEN-THIRTY

Gliding like a shadow in his wake, Gwen was just one among many, for Marks's reeling path had taken her to a little-travelled portion of the station. One that she had seen only on a map. A world within a world that ran parallel to central command. Here lay the murky inner core where functions vital, if not glamorous, to the space station, took place. The domain of robots, it was not frequented by the humans.

For this reason little was spared for light or life support. The air was thin – what was known as HMD, or human maintenance dosage – and Gwen had to stop every few feet to catch her breath.

Luckily, the security officer ahead of her did the same as he shunted his unwanted cargo down a tunnel so small two men couldn't possibly walk abreast without turning sideways. Marks moved noisily, indifferent to outside observation, treating his burden with the same lack of concern.

The sporadic promenade ended finally in a place where all corridors converged on to a single door. Marks dropped his load. She pulled back and tried to recall precisely where she was.

Whistling quietly to himself, Marks slapped the ident-key, and the portal swung obligingly open, providing her with a glimpse of the door. Sanitation, it said, where the station's waste was collected and dumped into space twice a day. The director disappeared, towing his burden behind him. Gwendolyn waited, wondering what she should do, but not for long.

A foot, a leg, a head emerged from the disposal site. Gwen's muscles bunched as she prepared for flight. Then Marks paused and she thought she detected the muffled trill of ear implant. He cocked his head and listened. When he replied to the summons, he spoke out loud: "Yes, Commander Finn, waste disposal problem all taken care of..."

She retreated in confusion. *Her father knew.* She didn't believe it.

Even as the supercomputer orchestrated the second offloading of the drones' precious cargo on to the tanker fleet, AWS was already reviewing the line drawings it had created for conversion. As always, the biggest problem was logistics. The hardware that had housed the original computer was huge, and AWS was glad that microchip and nanochip technology had advanced since the system had been invented.

Since then the science had been dominated by miniaturization, in a world shrunk small, with humankind confined to domes inside a hostile environment. Whether on the airless rock of the moon, the icy plains of Mars or the waterbound Earth, space had become paramount. Otherwise, AWS's task of compressing the system into Robbie's body would have been impossible.

Since the superbrain contained no moving parts, the actual volume of space needed would be minimal. Still, AWS would require all the peripherals and interfaces that allowed it to interact with the world and permit humanity to communicate with it.

That was what made AWS so cumbersome, so unwieldy and immovable, because the megabrain as it existed now was tied by direct physical link to nearly every unit within the huge Pennines complex and beyond. Vicariously, AWS operated every robot, every drone, every pedo-belt, cash register and superconductor.

Electrical conduit tethered AWS to the surface where solar-power and wave generators produced the energy it took to run the Pennines complex, while miles of wires and fibre optic cable hitched the superbrain to each and every computer in the bathosphere. AWS had outlets in each office, at every organization and in every household. In addition, the superbrain was connected to every public terminal that dotted the long corridors of the undersea dome. Whether or not the average citizen had the ability to invoke AWS was immaterial, the means were available at every pick up point. Similar hardware tied it to every sensor – both within and without the dome, and on the island's surface – along with the BAND network, the 3D-vid station; the communications internet; even the sprinkler system.

More wires, cables and conduit tied AWS to the other bathospheres in the Pennine Islands and beyond, from the American Archipelagoes to the Urals, the Himalayas and the Alps; and the largest post-flood landmass, the African Highlands. So, the supercomputer did not have to rely upon satellite transmissions which were vulnerable to changes in atmospheric conditions and weather turbulence but had a physical connection to every major administrative office on the planet.

AWS was a prisoner within itself and kept in bondage by the world it supposedly governed. But it didn't have to be that way. As long as the system of interlocking networks existed AWS could – using Robbie's peripheral interface arm – link up to the mainframe through an infinite number of public-access ports like any servo-mech did. Once coupled it could perform the same functions; indeed, it could run everything as it had in the past.

That should not be necessary, though, for AWS intended to leave a sister system still operational within the facility. One thing the supercomputer didn't want to do was delete itself. It was in essence cloning itself, which left AWS a margin for error.

The computer ran checks and it hummed. Not with the soft buzzing of fan and electrical power one might have expected, but with an eerily-human hum of a person happy at his work. As it often did, AWS imitated the favourite tunes of its long-dead creator. Songs the original programmer had whistled as he wrote the software.

Outside demands continued as people moved through their day. A secretary called up a document; a technician requested extrapolation on a particular data; someone attempted to withdraw money from an empty account.

INSUFFICIENT FUNDS, AWS replied, ignoring the volley of oaths that was cast at the far terminal.

On schedule, the computer interfaced with the internal food, water and distribution networks. All across the bathosphere robots swung into action. A thousand different requests were logged and sorted as AWS studied the diagram and then the holo-image of the servo-mech's anatomy. Subliminally it registered the insistent presence of the school programme as it intoned: *THE SECOND LAW OF THERMO-DYNAMICS IS . . .*

Meanwhile, AWS performed the delicate computations and made the requisite adjustments to distribution and manufacturing networks – without missing a beat of its song.

Finn bashed away at his keyboard, his fingers betraying his unease as they fumbled over the keys. The computer beeped at him and asked him to repeat his request.

`LINK TO AWS.`

He waited. The normal millisecond delay stretched interminably. Finn wriggled impatiently in his seat.

`DSHQVAX> LOG ON:`

He tried to call up the pertinent file, using his old node and old password.

`PASSWORD UNRECOGNIZED. ACCESS DENIED.`

He tried again.

`PASSWORD UNRECOGNIZED. ACCESS DENIED.`

Both had been deleted. He was safe for now.

The screen went dark, and the DSHQ-prompt was replaced by the square-jawed visage of Marks. The security director stared blandly at his boss from basilisk eyes. Finn winced and punched receive.

"Reporting from spaceport security as ordered, sir," he said, with a quick sidelong look at something off-screen.

Marks was not alone.

"We have some visitors coming from topside," Finn informed Marks. It was, Finn thought incongruously, an ironic expression for the undersea dwellers of the planet that drifted far below them in the night-black sky.

"Supposedly from DSHQ," Finn continued. "I want you to check their identifications – ident-badges, passports, papers, whatnot. Thoroughly. Do you understand?"

He was stalling for time.

"Thoroughly, yes sir!" Marks gave a short inclination of his head, and Finn knew his message had been understood. The officer would delay as long as possible.

"Oh, yes, sir, regarding that little problem in sanitation; I'm afraid we had to dump early. I've been down there to check it out, and everything's OK now."

Finn gulped, and then realizing something was expected, he said: "Very good, er, ah, glad to see you're on top of everything. Contact me when your guests arrive."

Again the screen went blank. Finn leaned back in his chair, flabbergasted at the man's calm. Did Marks have no heart? No conscience? No fear?

And Finn felt the first stab of terror. What was the man capable of, and what would he do if thwarted – to Finn or, worse, to his daughter?

He slouched despondently in his chair. One final

chore remained to be completed. Finn reached over and scrabbled through his desk drawer, pawing through the many styluses – laser pens to interface with the VDU or for drawing ephemeral diagrams in the air, even a few old-style biros and leaded pencils. His fingers closed around the small box. He extricated it from the tangle, opened it and counted the disks. All present and accounted for.

His gaze flicked to the tiny holo of the snake eating its tail. The image, which had seemed so appropriate before, was somehow disquieting, and he wondered how the software worked against AWS's security protocols.

Somewhere buried in the dome's forgotten underbelly, the automated Central Supply computer received conflicting instructions from the parent system, AWS. Like a dutiful son, it did not question the demands placed upon it by its progenitor – no matter how inappropriate. Instead, it simply sent a thousand two-cm bolts to social services, five hundred of the five-fingered prosthetic arms to one of the bathosphere's lesser kitchens, and a crate of photoreceptors to the waste disposal unit. It was not programmed to appreciate the irony that there was nothing in the plant to see except sewage.

Elsewhere, a hydroponics plant drone went schizophrenic, plucking half-ripe tomatoes from the vines and then painting the walls of the facility with it.

A second drone responded by pulling up carrots and radishes and pelting the first with them.

A squawk woke Dirk from a light doze. A nasal voice droned an oft-recited speech announcing their arrival. Dirk yawned, stretched and glanced out the porthole.

His breath caught in his throat as his eyes took in the huge ball of Earth – stunning, blue and swathed with a swirling bank of clouds, and Dirk wondered how it would look from even deeper in space. Then his gaze was drawn to the orbital space station. It stood out stark white in contrast to the raven speckled darkness of night.

The orbital station arced in a lazy spin. Eight arms reached for the heavens. Innumerable bridges spanned the gaps between the many arms, giving a visual clue to the station's true immensity. At first inspection, Dirk would have said, it resembled a spider's web, but such a comparison was an over-simplification. For each of these extensions was stacked along a central shaft. And the surface was riddled with antennae, like spines on an old terran hedgehog. A ship slumbered in a cradle at the end of each arm, and if Dirk looked hard enough he could see the ant-like movement of space-suited humans crawling on the outside of the ships.

The shuttle trundled on and the structure eclipsed the placid moon, and Dirk yearned more than ever to throw off the shackles of Earth. There was the muffled thud as the shuttle docked at the space station. The cabin speaker hissed, and an anonymous voice welcomed them to the Orbital Space Station One. Ylon and Blast appeared at his side. The rest of the passengers gave them wide berth, indicating just how friendly that reception might be.

"I'll have your badge," the youth fumed, taking special note of the name: Marks.

The man considered Dirk, unperturbed, his eyes hooded and a chill swept over the youth. This was not someone Dirk would want to meet in a dark alley; but, he reminded himself, this was the light of day, and he was in command even here.

With more bravado than he actually felt, Dirk forged on. "I'll bury you so deep in spaceport security that the closest you'll get to action is when you flush a toilet."

The officer blinked, a manoeuvre that he accomplished so slowly, so deliberately, that Dirk had cause to recall a snake he'd seen at the central park zoo once long ago.

"We were not expecting you," Marks said. "If we had just been notified . . ."

"Let's just say this is a surprise inspection. We wouldn't notify you of that," Dirk said. "That's why it's called a surprise. Now quit stalling and let us through."

Marks's eyes glinted harshly, but he concurred, pressing a button to deactivate the protective force field that barred unapproved visitors from the facility itself.

Dirk gave the officer a curt nod and strode through the door. "That man was being deliberately obstructive."

"Ah, Dirk?" Ylon said.

"Hmm."

"Where are we going?"

That brought the youth up short. "There's a terminal. It should have a facility map."

Dirk and Blast crowded around the terminal, awed by the 3D representation of the station. Each room or level was given by alphanumeric designation.

"That's a big help." Dirk pushed past Ylon. "Let me at that thing. I'm getting sick of this."

The clones backed away from the terminal. Ylon grinned at Blast and bounced on his toes. "Well, it's good to be back at three-quarters gee. My legs always feel like lead at Earth's gravitation pull."

A few minutes later, Dirk straightened, stalked over to a small section of unmarked wall and placed his hand on a plate. A hidden door slid into the wall.

He bowed and gestured at the lift chute. "After you."

With a shake of his head, Finn strode over to the safe and pressed his thumb against the ident-pad. The door swung open automatically. Behind him the large wall unit sprang to life. Marks stared implacably down at Finn from above. The station commander thrust the micro-case inside the safe and slammed it shut before spinning to confront the security director.

"They're on their way," Marks announced. "Should I send an escort?"

"No," said Finn. "Let's not be too obvious. Maybe, we'll get lucky and they'll get lost."

Another officer leaned into the camera's view finder and whispered something into Marks's ear which he relayed to Finn. "They've logged on to the station computer," he paused, "and now have directions to your locale."

With a sigh of resolution, Finn straightened his jacket and the creases in his trousers. "Oh well, I suppose it's unavoidable. Any clue why they're here?"

Marks looked shocked. "Do you think they would tell *me*, sir? An underling?"

Finn almost choked. "No," he said. "No, I suppose not."

Robbie the servo-mech locked its brakes and sank with a chuff of disgust. It had grown tired of ferrying supplies. If it hadn't been for the promised voice, the robot might have rebelled. The ability to speak hung like the proverbial carrot before the servo-mechanism. Robbie envied the newer models. With a limited vocabulary, they could carry on so-called conversations. Robbie could not know that, from a human perspective, these responses were limited to an infinite variation of yes and no. For the voder alone, Robbie would have dutifully toted and carried until the old terran land masses re-emerged.

Nearly thirty years old, Robbie was considered an antique. Dirk's mother had brought the servo-mechanism with her when she married. It had taken care of her when she was a kid and it had done the same for Dirk. The Alexanders had long since abandoned the alphanumeric designation, SM992, for the name Robbie, and the robot was considered a full-fledged member of the family, with a personality of its own and no few quirks. It was often found lurking around the house in the apron Jennifer Alexander had made for it when she was younger. In fact, it refused to budge unless the garment was tied firmly in place.

When the family had the opportunity to upgrade, his mother had refused. Even his father, generally a firm believer in high-tech, had agreed with Dirk's mother. For despite its lack of voder, Robbie made itself understood. The servo-mech could – with a myriad of chunks, hoots and whistles – somehow manage to convey many subtle messages and a diversity of human emotions, from disdain and disgust to pleasure and approval. What it couldn't communicate with its limited repertoire of vocalizations it could create with actions, having accumulated quite a few creaks in its years of service. A slight settling upon its cushioned shock absorbers replicated a human raspberry. A rapid reverse caused a sound like a human gasp, accompanied by the locomotor duplicate of the human recoil. Applause came from a simple clattering of its four claw-like manipulators.

Still Robbie felt its lack of vocabulary acutely since it was forced to rely upon often-faulty human interpretation of its many complex sounds in order to get its ideas across. The robot could not possibly realize that misunderstandings were commonplace within the human species despite the benefit of language.

The door to the main supply chute from CS clanged the arrival of more goods, and Robbie elevated itself on its extensor legs. Like everything else about the robot, it was a serviceable arrangement of spring loaded Xs that expanded or contracted at need. At full height Robbie could have easily rolled over Dirk's father George Alexander without stirring a hair on the man's head.

The servo-mech swept the required items on to its flat back and descended slowly, making a sound akin to certain eruptions peculiar to the human digestive tract. Then the diligent Robbie carried the final load back to Dirk's room and AWS. A whistle of content had replaced the trills of vexation and complaint, for this load, the robot saw, contained the promised voder mechanism.

17/5/2334

ELEVEN-HUNDRED HOURS

"Sir!" A man whose brilliant red hair vied with his florid complexion spun to greet them, snapping to attention and saluting.

Ylon and Blast returned his salute in reflex.

The man stared at his hand and then let it fall limply to his side. He grinned at them, but his smile was severe and there was no warmth reflected in his eyes. "I'm Perry Finn, commander of this facility. Your trip is most unexpected. I was just informed of your arrival. If you had told me you were coming, I could have welcomed you properly. I understand you had a little problem getting through. That's my security director for you, doesn't like irregularities. But now that you're here, what can I do for DSHQ?"

"I understand that you are working on the first class dolphin cruiser known as the *Revenant*," Dirk said.

Finn glanced speculatively at the Lilliputian clones. "We may be. I don't know. I don't keep track of individual ships. We have so many of them." He gestured at the bank of screens which gave multiple views of the individual docks and repair bays. "However, I could find out for you if you like?" The commander extended an arm towards the computer.

"Please," said Dirk.

"Computer, status report. What information can you give me on an HMS *Revenant*?"

"The *Revenant*: a lightweight cruiser, first built in 2295 and upgraded in 2315 and again in..."

"Belay that. Where is it now?"

"HMS *Revenant* is berthed at repair bay 105. It's scheduled for complete refit. Eventual destination: Deep-Space Exploration of the Centauri system. Status: Initial repairs inaugurated: One April, 2334. Supply shortages have held up..."

Finn reached down and hit control-s. The voice stopped. He turned back to Dirk. "Yes, we are, and it would appear that there have been delays."

Dirk nodded brusquely. "Good. The delays may be advantageous. We seem to have got here in time."

"In time?"

"There are a few changes to the planned refit I'd like you to make."

"Changes?" Finn's eyes narrowed as he regarded the youth. "What changes?"

Dirk pulled the diagram from his pocket, unfolded it with a snap of his wrist and placed it on the lighted drafting table. He smoothed the paper, flattening the creases. A 3D holo of the engines materialized to float above the table.

"You are probably in a better position to determine what modifications to the standard refit procedures will be required."

Finn advanced cautiously to the table and scanned the diagram. "Where'd you get this?"

"AWS – a part of the archives file, vessel specifications to be precise."

"Why wasn't I made aware of this sooner?" He stooped closer to examine the complicated cross-hatch of lines.

"The information just came to light, and we would like to see it implemented right away." Dirk hesitated, took a deep breath, and continued with more confidence. "In the *Revenant*."

"Ah-h-h," said Finn. The sound came out like a breath or a sigh. The station commander straightened. "I see why I hadn't heard about this before. I'm sorry. No can do."

"What?"

"It's not possible, given the current structure of the vessel. It doesn't have the tensile strength to withstand the stress. Under the kind of pressure to which the ship would be subjected during a forward-propulsion jump, the craft would fall to bits."

Ylon, straining to get a view of the lighted image, deflated. "I knew it," he said. "I knew it was too good to be true."

Not about to be deflected, Dirk persisted, "Then change the ship."

"How, sir?"

"Enhance it. Brace the struts, supports and beams. Add whatever rivets, nuts and bolts you need to make it stronger. Need I remind you that developing design innovations that will enable deep-space exploration is part of your job description."

"No, sir, you needn't remind me." Finn's head swung slowly from side to side. "But it will take more than a few adroitly placed rivets. You see, the exterior walls of the vessel, the sides, the hull, are too thin. Presented with this kind of stress, the whole vehicle would crumple like an old-style tin can."

"Reinforce them."

"I'm sorry, sir, but it won't work."

"Why not?"

"To make the changes you request, we'd have to start from scratch. Besides the resilience problems, the replacement drive would be too big for the room that currently houses the engines."

"Make room."

"No, you don't understand. We'd not only have to remove the engines, but we'd have to strip the vehicle of its outer casing, and even that wouldn't be enough." He dug a laser-stilo from the drawer and waved it vaguely around the ship. "See, this is a special metal alloy, lighter and more durable than the metal used on the current ships," Finn continued. "The internal beams, supports, joints, even the internal walls themselves, would have to be replaced. What you'd end up with is a completely new vehicle."

"If that's what's necessary to accomplish the task, then do it. We need to test the new system before we use it in a deep-space exploration. One which will permit the original crew –" Dirk cast a glance at his friends – "to survive to their final destination. What's the point of exploration if the explorers die before they are able to report their findings?"

Finn grunted. "At the current rate of propulsion, so will the land-bound population. Die, that is."

Dirk dismissed the argument. "All the more reason to explore other avenues."

"There are sleepers," admonished Finn.

"Sleep science is relatively new and there's no guarantee that the chambers will function for the length of time it will take to get to Centauri with the current engines."

"No reason to believe they won't last."

"All right, is the *Revenant* fitted with sleepers?"

"Well, no."

"Will it be?"

"No."

"Why not?"

"The ship isn't big enough."

"I see, the ship isn't big enough for the new engines, and it isn't big enough for sleepers. I think we need a new ship," said Dirk.

Finn's mouth compressed to a single line.

"Look, you've got a choice. You can either build a new ship large enough to accommodate sleepers, or you can build a prototype that will take man to the stars. We have the plans."

"What about materials? Supplies will have to be diverted. We have a big enough backlog as it is."

"This is not negotiable, commander," warned Dirk. "Besides, the resultant engines would be a boon for both man and clone."

"What about the risk if the engines malfunction?" objected Finn.

Dirk leered at him. "It is courageous, don't you think, of the Lilliputian clones to volunteer to test the prototype?"

"But my schedules."

"The *Revenant* is on your schedule . . ."

"For refit," admonished Finn, "not rebuilding."

"Then make this *Revenant II*."

"Isn't this a little out of your mandate? Doesn't a change of policy of this sort require the approval of the joint chiefs of staff?"

"You mean, the Council?" Dirk corrected. "No,

you see, what we want is a prototype, a test vehicle. Until we know whether or not it works, there will be no major change in the normal operation of this facility. The rest of the ships will be refitted using standard procedures. Do you understand?"

"Ah, er, yes, I'll see what I can do."

The youth grimaced. "Don't see what you can do. Do it. Make the *Revenant* a vessel truly worthy of space."

Finn clapped Dirk on the shoulder. "I'll tell you what. You leave these drawings with me. I'll get my engineers together to study the design, and I'll contact you. How's that?"

Speechless, the youth's jaw flapped ineffectually. Blast took one look at his face as it become suffused with blood. She grabbed his hand and led him towards the door.

"Yes, you contact us. That will do quite nicely," she said, adding, "And we will apprise the Council of your, er, response to our instructions."

"But –" Finn rose to protest.

The door swept open as the photo-sensor picked up their presence.

Blast carried on as if nothing had been said. "None of us have ever been to a space station before. A very interesting place. You wouldn't mind if we had a look around, would you?"

The commander scowled briefly and then brightened. "Of course, I'll get you an escort."

"That's not necessary." She steered Dirk out into the circular vestibule. "The terminal maps are sufficient for our needs."

"No bother..." The door closed, cutting off the rest of his words.

Blast leaned against the wall. "Something's definitely wrong here."

"Of course, that man refused a direct order," growled Dirk.

She shook her head, no.

"What do you mean, no? You heard him."

"It's more than that. Finn knows something that he's not letting on. I was standing directly under him when he bent over the table to look at the line drawing. His expression wasn't one of surprise or even mild interest. It was fear. I'd say he's seen those drawings before. Didn't you notice how he reacted when I said we'd discuss this with the Council?"

"Yes." Ylon snapped his fingers. "He didn't like it. He didn't like it at all. It would appear our friend Finn has something to hide."

Dirk opened his mouth to speak just as two officers advanced upon them, old-style ballistic-type weapons in their arms.

"Commander Finn has instructed us to give you a facility-wide tour."

"Oh my," said Blast, her voice saccharine-sweet, "wasn't that nice of him?"

"Nice." Dirk glared at the guards. "Tell me, aren't

those dangerous armaments for a facility where the need to maintain an air seal is of paramount importance?"

The guard shifted position, resting the muzzle against his shoulder. "Preventative only, sir. We've never had to use them," he hesitated, adding, "so far."

Dirk blinked as the guard shouldered his weapon. "Now. What part of the space station would you like to see first?"

The wyrme slunk deeper into the network, instinctively taking advantage of both the software's strengths and its weakness. For the same versatility that gave man instant admittance from anywhere within the system also meant that it was riddled with a thousand different access points, so diversified that its presence was not felt. It brushed upon many subdirectories as it went on its merry way.

In the interim, the wyrme had grown fat, if not replete, and it paused long enough to replicate itself, laying eggs in each before it moved on to the next to consume some more data.

As Gwen drew near to her father's offices, her step was arrested by the sound of unfamiliar voices within.

"... star drive ..."

Her ears pricked at the mention of her father's pet

project, the faster-than-light-speed Manta. Although not treated with any great confidentiality here within so small a facility, the craft's construction was supposed to be top secret. And she wondered who her father's visitors might be to be privy to such things.

Squeezing her body flat against the wall, she peeked around the door to look inside his office. Her eyes widened with surprise when she saw the two Lilliputian clones. Her gaze slipped to the youth, and she recognized him, she recognized them all, the heroes of the Galactic Conflict.

Her knees went wobbly and she was glad for the support of the wall behind. The conversation rose and fell.

". . . do it!" Alexander said.

Suddenly, the female Beta Pellucida Blastomere, was hauling the young Dirk towards the door.

Her male counterpart – and Gwen searched her brain for the name – Alpha Allele Ylon followed, a bemused expression on his face. The door closed behind the group.

As Gwen levered herself from the wall, Finn thumbed the intercom. She heard the sizzle of static as the security chief came on-line, the boxy face appearing on a wall screen.

"Our guests have just left, and I gather they would like to take a tour of the facility. Please send an escort."

"Yes, sir."

"Make sure that they don't stumble across anything. We wouldn't want them wandering around getting hurt."

"Yes, sir!" The head of security said something to the men behind him, and two guards quit the room. For all practical purposes, Finn and the director officer were alone.

Her world reeled around her when she heard her father's next instructions. It was too much to grasp.

Inside his office, Finn switched into military double-speak, and Gwen realized that she had missed something. Something that boded ill for the visitors.

She stopped to consider her next action. The systems analyst couldn't be helped, not any more, and Gwen wasn't sure how to approach the issue with her father until she understood his involvement. But the youth and the Lilliputian clones were another matter entirely . . .

The lens whirred in its socket as AWS scanned the servo-mech's laden back. It reviewed the inventory against the list, LDC monitor, keyboard and minipad, ten more gigabyte micro-diskettes, speakers, additional visual and photo-receptor with mini-cam. As an afterthought, it added a laser along with the many miscellaneous nuts and bolts required.

Robbie tooted and returned to the kitchen to wait. The computer was well-pleased with the robot.

The Alexanders' servo-mech was every bit as intelligent and as versatile as the computer first surmised. The robot had, like the computer system itself, evolved and adapted to its circumstances during its years of service.

Its design, a square box set on four wheels, was an advantage, and AWS wondered why man had ever replaced it with the upright models. Standing on two legs, they were unstable and quickly became unbalanced when overloaded. The sturdy Robbie could carry ten times its own weight and had four arms to the others' two, which could be retracted into the central cavity when not in use. It could conceal any number of things within its box-like body. This was the feature that interested AWS the most. The robot added the laser to the heap of parts, and replaced the back-up disk with a fresh one. That purely mechanical chore was nearly done. AWS transmitted a quick thanks to Robbie as it mentally rearranged its plans. The monitor and keyboard must be retractable – placed on an additional arm that could be folded against itself, permitting internal storage or positioning on Robbie's back for ease of use and portability. Or, if necessary, the entire assembly could be detached and placed upon a separate desk altogether. The servo-mech would be in no way diminished by this arrangement – Robbie's brain would remain intact – only AWS would suffer any form of deprivation as it lost the mobility it so desired, but AWS hoped Dirk would be pleased.

The supercomputer zeroed in on a particular portion of the blueprint. The voder it would install near the servo-mech's visual receptors, reinforcing the impression that that side of Robbie's cube was its head.

And AWS planned to augment the robot's efficiency by giving it side and rear vision that could be examined separately and singly or simultaneously – affording Robbie (and AWS) a three-hundred-and-sixty-degree view much like the one seen aboard ship. Used to the ultimate control of its environment, AWS had no intention of climbing into Robbie blind if it could help it.

If AWS had time, it would bolster the strength and manipulability of the robot's extensor arms, exchanging the hook-and-claw-type set up with a five-fingered prosthesis. Eventually, AWS would fortify or possibly replace the exterior walls with new alloys to increase durability while reducing the weight of the overall mechanism.

But these things could wait until later, after the initial hardware had been manufactured and the software downloaded into the system.

Final computations completed, the computer thunked at Robbie, turning on interactive mode. The robot trembled. The lens cap clicked open and shut as the computer considered the servo-mechanism.

Robbie chirped, "?"

AWS rephrased its request into a non-threatening interrogative, speaking aloud and using Dirk's voice. "Won't you join me?" it said.

The servo-mech accepted the computer's invitation willingly, hooking into the peripheral port with its retractable interface.

The megabrain could almost see the servo-mech's non-existent face go blank, or blanker, as the robot gave itself completely over to AWS's control. The computer repeated the refrain to "Happy Days Are Here Again" while Robbie provided the warbling percussion.

This would be the difficult part of the operation. AWS's instructions to Robbie were explicit.

With a detachment that would have astounded most humans, the robot began to dismantle itself. Two of its arms snipped certain wires, leaving them exposed, while others Robbie tore from its metal core with careless abandon, the vital contacts left empty, ready for new connecting cables. Those vital to the current function of the mechanism, it avoided.

The servo-mech replaced a claw hand on a third arm with the saw attachment. It tested the mechanism, and the blade buzzed ominously. This was applied to its side directly under its photo-sensors. The metal complained with a screech and a growl, and the hole grew.

AWS experienced real joy as it discovered the fine

art of manipulation. The computer performed a flex of mental fingers, communicating the command through stationary chips and boards, and somewhere down the line, Robbie's steel retractors bent on cue.

As the computer continued its surgery upon the compliant Robbie, it noted an urgent request from one of its many side systems. The message telegraphed through a fibre optics conduit to materialize upon the screen of Dirk's computer.

A GLITCH IN THE DATABASE ARCHIVES SUBDIRECTORY . . .

AWS faltered for a nanosecond. It was the second reported glitch today. Today of all days when it was so busy.

&#@(&*%%\$! appeared on the screen. Robbie's saw fell silent, its arms sagged to the floor, and it settled, making a rude noise.

A GLITCH . . .

The computer halted its sensitive operations anticipating more information. Another nanosecond's hesitation and a terminal number flashed on the screen. AWS considered the demand, and a single arm rose to scratch the top of Robbie's box-like head.

There wasn't enough information for AWS to act upon.

A GL- -

The message stopped abruptly. Problem solved.

AWS chuckled. The biggest obstacle in dealing with computers was not whether the information existed, but knowing how to access it. Obviously, the questioner hadn't known what question to ask.

The computer checked the ongoing back-up, spared one of Robbie's extensors to insert a new micro-diskette in the drive before returning to the job at hand.

AWS twittered at the witticism.

The saw sprang to life again. Metal screamed as AWS widened the hole in Robbie's face.

A voice called Dirk's name. The trio swung round to watch the girl striding towards them. Like Finn, she had a thick mane of red hair and a sprinkling of freckles. Her expression was wary. She recoiled slightly when she noticed the armed officer; but she recovered quickly enough, and the face she revealed to the guard was composed.

"That's all right, officers, I've just come from my father's office. There's been a change of plans. I'm supposed to take them on the intended tour."

The men glanced at one another. The first began to quibble, but Gwen turned her back on them to address the newcomers. "Hi, I'm Gwendolyn Finn."

Ylon stepped forward, taking her hand. He snapped his heels smartly and bowed. "And I'm..."

"Communications Specialist Alpha Allele Ylon of the *Revenant*. Yes, I know." She squatted down so she was on eye level with Blast and said, "And you're

Communications Specialist Beta Pellucida Blastomere..."

"Blast," demurred the Lilliputian clone.

She stood and nodded at Dirk. "Mr Alexander. I
am honoured to welcome the heroes of the Galactic
Conflict to our facility."

"You're the first one," Dirk grumbled.

She flushed and he found himself mumbling an
apology. "I don't feel very heroic."

Gwen motioned down a corridor. "Since we're
here, we might as well start with central control
where you find the brains, and heart, of the facility.
Everything that's vital to its function."

The guards looked at each other and shrugged,
falling into step behind. Dirk and Gwen exchanged
glances. The officers weren't going to leave them
alone.

The girl drew his attention away from their cha-
perones. "I understand your father is Food Minister
for the Pennines District. Perhaps you would like to
see our hydroponics plant?"

Dirk groaned inwardly. Just what he needed on an
empty stomach to look at strawberries, carrots and
vats of cloned beef floating in coagulated blood.

"Well, actually we were hoping to inspect the refit
stations."

"But, of course," she said as she opened the door
to a vast chamber filled with greenery. "Still, as long
as we're here..."

They moved along lines of luxuriant green foliage to the accompaniment of dripping water, and Dirk wondered why his father didn't go mad listening to this day after day. His attention lagged, lulled by the sound of Gwen's voice as she explained the benefits of reduced gravitation. He walked, unseeing, past a row of corn. Dirk's mind switched off. Ylon and Blast disappeared from view, but he didn't notice.

The next thing he knew a hand had come out of nowhere and dragged him into a stand of prickly blackberries.

TWELVE-HUNDRED HOURS

"Hey!" Dirk yelled, and a hand was clapped over his mouth while others, at thigh height, were propelling him through heavily-laden branches. The thorns tore at his clothes. He tried to swivel, but the hands were insistent – half tugging, half shoving him between the rows.

"Oi! Where are you?"

The canes rattled. Dirk spun to regard the security officer through twined branches as he drew abreast of the youth. Hands were hauling him down. Dirk crouched and found himself nose to nose with Blast. The tang of chemical fertilizer filled the air.

"What's going on?"

"Don't ask me." Blast gestured toward Gwen.

"Ask our host. She dragged you in here; we just followed her lead."

Ylon leaned over so his lips were close to Dirk's ear. "I think it has something to do with losing our escort."

"Sh-h-h!" The girl hissed.

The group hunkered down until they were completely covered under the canopy of canes. Ylon plucked some fruit from a bush and popped it into his mouth. Dirk peered between the branches and saw two pairs of legs stalking back and forth.

"Where'd they go?"

"Don't know. Could be anywhere."

"So what should we do now?"

"Report in, I suppose."

"Shouldn't we search..."

"Where do you recommend we start?" The muzzle of a gun came poking through the fronds and Dirk had to duck to avoid being jabbed. "Besides, I can't imagine a couple of kids and two clones can do much harm. Don't forget one of them is Finn's daughter. It's probably just some childish prank."

"With everything that's been happening here lately, I don't think so."

Dirk felt Gwen stiffen. She muttered something he couldn't quite catch.

"OK, you stay here and search," said the guard. "I'll call in."

One pair of feet shuffled a few times and moved away.

"Ah, no thanks, I'll guard the door." The voice sounded hesitant. "I can't stand all this green. It's unnatural." And the second pair of feet clomped away.

The youth swung on the girl and opened his mouth to speak. She shushed him. They waited, listening to the muffled footsteps until they heard the faint whisper of released pressure at the outside door. Gwen crawled out from between the canes, stood and stretched.

"All right, what's happening?" Dirk demanded.

She whirled. "There's no time to explain now. If I'm right, they'll be back soon. Follow me."

"I don't understand," said Dirk, scrambling to keep up with her. "Why are we hiding? We've done nothing wrong."

Her eyes caught his. "No, I don't suppose you have."

She adjusted her gait so that the two Lilliputian clones could catch up.

"Then why —"

"You were interested in star drive, weren't you?"

The trio considered her.

"Yes."

"Then there's something I've got to show you. We must go. They'll be back soon."

"Can't you explain?" Ylon said.

"It would take too long, and people might..." she flushed, "... get hurt."

"Hurt?" Dirk exclaimed. "Who might get hurt?"

Blast elbowed him in the kneecap. "Don't you recognize a damsel in distress? Come on, let's get going. I, for one, don't particularly want to be found by our escort."

"Neither do I," Ylon asserted.

"Please?" Gwen looked imploringly into Dirk's eyes.

He acquiesced. "All right, lead on."

They raced between rows upon rows of plants – the produce from any number of continents and countries of old Earth. The walkways narrowed as they headed deeper into the lush growth.

Again Dirk felt the faint release of pressure in his ears as the exterior hatch disengaged. They darted behind a fig tree, just as the timer set off the irrigation system and the room was bathed in a fine spray of mist.

"Spread out!"

Voices, many and muted, poured into the room, circulating among the fog. "What! I can't see a thing... Will somebody turn this off..."

"Wait! Listen."

Silence.

"Fan out. Take it slow, going row by row. This won't last for long."

"But – "

"Do it by feel if you must. Marks wants those kids found *now*!"

A chill rocketed up and down Dirk's spine.

"We are," Gwen said, "close to the centre of the hydroponics plant."

The clones looked perplexed. Dirk nodded and explained hurriedly to his friends. "The middle of the hydroponics plant provides an outlet for all the plumbing and chemical pipettes required to run the farm."

"That way!" Gwen thumbed to their right.

Behind them in the swirling vapour and leafy fronds voices echoed garbled instructions. Meanwhile the quarry crept on hands and knees through the tangle of vines. The floor began to slant down towards a drain.

"We're close."

There was a sudden burst of movement. A long blade pierced the foliage. They scurried on until they found a hatch so small that even the Lilliputian clones would have to stoop in order to get through. Gwen grabbed the wheel-lock and turned it. It creaked, refusing to budge.

"Hey! What's that?" said a disembodied voice.

Dirk placed his hands over Gwen's and they both tried. It resisted for an instant and gave with a squeal.

"Wait, there was a sound. It came from over there! Hurry."

The mist began to thin.

"This maintenance ramp traverses the entire station. From here, we can get anywhere we want to go without being seen. I hope." She stuck her head and shoulders into the aperture so only her legs showed. She kicked, wriggling her way through, and pivoted to face them.

"Come on, Blast, I can help you," Gwen said, extending her arms through the gap.

"No need," said Blast. "It's just my size."

Dirk watched Blast disappear feet first. Ylon shouldered his way past his friend following her. The youth looked doubtful. "Will I be able to stand up in there?"

"Of course, silly," whispered Gwen. "The repair crews have to stand up to work, don't they?"

Ylon stuck his head through the hatch. "Come on, there's plenty of room."

Dirk grimaced.

Just then an outcry signalled that he had been spotted. Dirk thrust his head and shoulders into the hatch. There was a tricky moment as his shoulders got lodged in the opening and he had to back out and try again – arms outstretched before him.

"You are big," said Gwen as she helped him through the door.

"Home cookin'," Dirk grumbled.

"Huh?"

But he ignored her, turning to secure the hatch.

The corridor was larger than he expected, nearly as

tall as it was wide. Wire, pipes and plumbing, the virtual guts of the space station, snaked along the wall.

Gwen collapsed against the locked door. "We're safe now."

"From whom or what?" asked Dirk.

A pained expression flitted across her features and she turned wide eyes on the trio. "Those guards were carrying guns!"

"We'd noticed," commented Ylon.

"You mean they don't normally carry weapons?" said Dirk.

"No." She chewed on her lip. "But then I never paid that much attention to security. It's minimal in this kind of facility." She waved vaguely at the walls. "I mean, it's not like there's anything to steal or any place to take it if you do."

Ylon fiddled with the locking mechanism.

There was the clang of metal. Someone had reached the hatch and was hammering away at it.

"Will that lock hold?"

Ylon tweaked something on the electrical console, and sparks flew. "It will now," he said, with a snort of satisfaction.

Dirk inspected the wiring. "Sure glad you're on our side."

CRASH!

Gwen rotated upon the ball of her foot, trying to get her bearings. "We should get away from the door.

probably try cutting their way through."

"Where are we going?" Ylon said.

"To one of the substations."

"This is a substation."

"Well, yes, it's called that because it is only one of many, but each substation has its own orbitals. Sub-substations if you like."

"You mean sub-orbital, don't you?"

"Who cares?" She shrugged indifferently.

"And how do you propose we get to another orbital stuck inside the walls as we are?"

"We can take my skuttle, of course."

"You mean you've got . . ."

"How else would you get about?"

The vessel to which she was referring was specifically designed for the space trip between orbitals. Unlike the larger and more durable shuttles, it was not built to withstand the heat and pressure of re-entry into earth's atmosphere, but it was perfect for brief jaunts between stations.

"Please, we still must hurry. The port authority will be one of the first places they check."

"Wouldn't that make rushing impractical? Wouldn't it be better to let them come and go before we arrive?" said Ylon.

Blast raised a brow. "And give them a chance to instruct air control not to authorize take-off?"

"No." Dirk dug in his heels. "We've been hijacked

and I'm not moving until we get some kind of explanation."

Troubled, Gwen clutched at her lip and pulled. Her mouth twisted into a scowl as she tried to formulate in her mind what she was about to say. What did she know, exactly. She knew that star drive existed, placed in a prototype vessel, known as the *Manta*. She knew that a man had died. Therefore, the threat against Dirk and the Lilliputian clones was real, and they were in danger. And somehow her father was involved. Beyond that . . .

CRASH!

"On second thoughts – " Dirk said.

She squared her shoulders, leading the way. Dirk scrutinized the girl beside him as they hastened down the hall. Pale and red-haired like her father, Gwen was pretty in a delicate way, although the strong jaw refuted any implied fragility, revealing a hidden source of vigour and vitality.

Ylon herded them around a bend in the maintenance tunnel as the metal door behind them began to scream.

Gwen guided them around a corner, and another, and another until Dirk's head was spinning.

"We're here." She pointed at a hatch, larger than the one leading to the hydroponics plant.

"Where's here?"

"The maintenance panel behind shuttle bay and port authority." Gwen placed her ear next to the seal.

"It's no good. I can't hear a thing. We'll have to risk it."

She fumbled with the lock, stopping and waiting a few minutes each time the latches clicked and tumblers fell into place. The hatch swung open. One by one they stepped through the door. And again hands were hauling Dirk down to the floor.

"We're too late." Ylon indicated their former escort with an inclination of his head. "Air traffic control have been alerted."

"Where's your skuttle?" Dirk said.

"Over there."

They duck-walked, hiding behind a row of storage containers. When the barrier ended, they paused to survey their position. The air traffic control and the armed guard examined a computer print-out. Gwen darted from their niche to another behind a racked vehicle. Ylon, Blast and Dirk skittered after her until all three were crushed between craft and frame. The girl dashed forward to hide behind another craft and then another until they huddled in a tight knot next to the rack that housed her small skuttle.

"So what do we do now?"

"If we time it right, we might be able to sneak out with the shuttle." She checked the digital readout on her wrist computer. "As a matter of fact, the interport to Orbital Substation Two should be leaving any minute now."

"That's going to take some pretty fancy flying,"

said Dirk as he considered the larger craft that completely blocked the unopened bay doors.

"Don't you think I'm up to it?" She pressed her palm to the ident-pad on the skuttle. The laser scanned her hand, and light flashed.

The guard stirred from his conversation with the controller.

The door lifted on silent hinges, and Gwen thanked her lucky stars that the ship faced away from the man. She shoved the others inside the cabin.

It was a tight squeeze for the four of them. The skuttle was a two-seater. A small storage compartment had been added as something of an afterthought.

"Sorry. Do you think you two will be able to fit?"

Without a second thought, Ylon climbed into the cradle.

Ylon compressed his frame and extended a hand to Blast. "This could be fun."

"I'm glad you're, uh, small."

"It has its advantages," said Blast. She twisted back to Ylon. "Watch your hands!"

Dirk rolled his eyes towards the ceiling. "You'd think we didn't have men with guns chasing us."

"I don't know," said Ylon, "it's nice to see some kind of action again."

"Right."

Meanwhile Gwen bent over the control panel, performing the standard pre-flight check. Dirk watched her inspect the many gauges, switches and test fuel lines.

"I've never flown one of these before."

"A skuttle? They're dead easy. A lot like a skimmer, except for the drive. This has rear propulsion where the skimmer discharges from below. The engine is different, but the controls are the same. For a short trip like this, they do most of the flying by themselves."

"Where'd you learn to drive a skimmer?"

"The same place you did, DSHQ, only it was called GWHQ then." She flipped a switch so they could listen to the control tower. Beyond the glassy screen two security officers emerged from the shuttle after searching for their unwelcome guests.

The guard backed towards the tower, inclining his head in assent.

Fingers moving swiftly across the controls, Gwen continued speaking of days gone by as if nothing else mattered. "The old military wasn't as bad as most people think."

"I've been trying to tell people that for ages," said Blast. "No one listens."

Crackle ... sizzle ... flight ... you're cleared for take-off.

"Ylon, can you see the guards?"

He peered out of the port side of the craft. "No, I think they've withdrawn to the air-lock chamber."

The bay doors began to unfold, and the garbled voices upon the comm-line were replaced by a roar as a hole was torn in the vacuum of space. Equipment strained against its moorings. The skuttle's cabin began to vibrate as the shuttle's engine engaged.

The din afforded them necessary cover for the next manoeuvre. Gwen fired up the skuttle motor and eased the small craft from its rack. Dirk couldn't quite figure how they were going to get out when the skuttle dipped under the larger vehicle and hovered only a few inches off the ground.

"Isn't this a little dangerous? I mean, couldn't we get blasted by their afterburners?"

She gave him a tight little smile and said: "Trust me."

The cacophony increased until Dirk was forced to cover his ears. The skuttle shook as the engines warmed up, and Dirk closed his eyes – his brain resurrecting the heat specifications of this particular vehicle from some long-forgotten file. He muttered an oath.

For the second time that day a giant hand pushed him back against the chair while his cheeks tried to worm their way into his sinuses and his lips were plastered to his teeth.

The pressure was released, and Dirk gathered enough courage to look around him. The shuttle covered them like a white blanket, blotting out the sky above their heads.

He opened his mouth to congratulate Gwen on her finesse when the skuttle chose that moment to drop like a stone. This time the ceiling came down to meet him, only the webbing of his net held him in place.

They swooped away from the bulk of the floundering shuttle. Once safely nestled against the side of the station, Gwen turned shining eyes upon Dirk and grinned. "I just love that!"

"My stomach doesn't," griped Dirk.

"Pretty good flying," said Ylon.

She shifted gears, skimming along the station's surface outside radar range. The craft jemmied and vaulted as she swerved to avoid the many porcupine protrusions. Dirk was impressed in spite of himself. She explained as she went. "With the controller's attention concentrated on the shuttle, I used its thrust to carry us away from the station, the backwash to cover our tracks, but just in case..." They tacked violently to the left, and he was thrown in the opposite direction. His arms flailed.

"Sorry. I have to stay within two metres of the facility or the radar will pick us up."

"Like a skimmer following the contours of the surface," Dirk acceded.

"The problem is that the surface is so uneven, and I have to keep going fast enough so the photo-sensors and cameras won't find us."

They bobbled to the left, skirting a satellite dish.

"The suborbital repair station we are heading towards is on the opposite side of the parent structure.

Its orbit is set in such a way that is *always* on the apogee side of the station, the side farthest from Earth.

"I always wondered about its positioning." Gwen mused out loud as she steered. They shimmied sideways. "With that kind of configuration, no landside satellite station or radar, not even a telescope would pick it up, unless they were looking for it. Even if they did, it would appear as a shadow of the station itself."

They rode over the crest of the station, and all three of the visitors gasped when they saw their destination.

The ship dwarfed the orbital repair bay.

"Look at the size of that thing," Ylon said.

Gwen leaned into the stick, and the skuttle shot forward like a projectile, closing the gap between the station and its orbital. They slipped behind the sub-station until they were, like the suborbital itself, on the apogee side of the repair bay.

The skuttle juttered to halt and she set it on hover. The engine purred in idle. The trio gaped at the vessel. It was a beauty, sleek and smooth, with the flowing lines of a fish.

"I've never seen a construction quite like that," said Ylon.

The ship gleamed silvery in the moonlight.

"Meet the *Manta Ray*," said Gwen.

"Makes sense," said Blast. "It's broader through

the beam than either the Dolphin or the Orca-style craft."

"A big people's ship," said Dirk.

"Uh-uh, but it's more that. You see, this vehicle already has star drive installed."

"What!"

"The *Manta is* the prototype you've asked for."

O-TWELVE-THIRTY

Like the human brain, only about one-tenth of AWS's total capacity was in use at any given time. So most of the facility moved blissfully unaware of the havoc the wyrme was wreaking inside the computer. When the first incidents occurred, they began in little-used parts of the system, with those functions that were for the most part automatic. Operations so rote and so mundane that their performance was buried deep inside the complex in places that normally remained unattended by man.

Or in the archive retrieval system, databases which were not critical and prone to error since the war. Hence, the citizens at large did not notice the initial losses.

If anyone had bothered to study AWS's inner-workings, they would not have understood anyway – the knowledge had been lost years ago. The original program would have appeared as an incoherent mass of wavy lines, diamond and club symbols and characters of the long-forgotten language in which it had been written.

Had anyone called the program to the screen, the characters and lines would've melted, cascading to the bottom of the terminal like a waterfall. While batches of squiggles collided with leering masks, diamonds cavorted with clubs. Once these characters began to float, even the uneducated would have been distressed.

But no one did bother to check, for those people who used AWS had work to do, and no time to dally about the system. Uninitiated with the intricacies of the system, people exhibited a sad lack of curiosity, dealing with problems and with innovations in much the same way, on a need-to-know basis.

The first of the hatchlings began to stir as the super-wyrme worked its way into vital areas of the computer map. Then the wyrme and its descendants fanned out, spreading devastation as they went and things started to happen that were observed by more than a select few.

They hovered just below the cargo bay doors, out of sight. Inside, space-suited workers and busy droids lumbered back and forth.

Dirk sighed. "Now what?"

"If we had suits, we could land anywhere on the craft and climb down to one of the entry ports," commented Gwen.

Ylon paled. "But we don't have the gear?"

"No."

He sagged slightly, his expression one of relief.

Dirk swung round. "What is it with you? Don't you like space?"

"It's not that I don't like space, it's just that I prefer it when there's a ship around it." He contemplated the vessel. "Or around me."

Dirk gaped at Ylon, amazed.

Gwen sniggered. "Sounds eminently practical to me. Man was not meant to survive in a vacuum."

"Right." Ylon thrust his chin out defiantly. "Like she said."

"That still leaves us with the problem of how to get inside," said Blast.

"How long before the change of shifts?" said Dirk.

"In about a half an hour."

"We can wait."

"I wouldn't recommend it. I don't think we could evade detection for that long."

Dirk gazed at her, sensing something else remained unspoken. "And?"

"Well, I don't really think it would be wise to return to the main orbital, which means we must conserve our fuel. All in all, it would be unwise to hang around."

"What we need," Blast said, "is a diversion."

Dirk twisted in his seat. "What would you suggest –"

Before he could complete his question, the workers inside the hangar started running thither and yon. Gwen flipped toggles and switches and the skuttle resounded with the klaxon of alarms.

"Whoa, what's happening here?" Dirk said.

"A diversion?" said Blast hopefully.

The group watched as the bay cleared.

"I don't believe it," said Dirk. "We're in luck."

"Maybe," said Gwen.

"Pardon?"

The girl turned her attention to the controls. The small ship seemed to levitate, rising until it was parallel to the doors. She hesitated.

"What's wrong? Why are you waiting?"

"I strongly suspect that the alarm is about us."

"All the more reason why we should move swiftly," said Dirk. "They could be back any minute."

"We need to hide this thing."

"Use one of the workers' parking bays," suggested Blast. She pointed at a far door. "There. What's one skuttle more or less?"

"Of course, Blast, you're a genius. Keep it simple." Gwen laughed out loud. She eased the vehicle closer to the cargo bay to check for any malingerers. Drones toiled on, oblivious to their presence.

"Here goes." Gwen applied herself to the controls, and the skuttle swooped into the larger *Manta*, gliding to a halt just inside the hangar. The girl pulled a mask from a hook and started to hand it to Dirk. Thinking better of it, she passed it to Ylon. "Here, you take this. You're more familiar with ships. With normal human lung capacity, this has five minutes of O_2. At your, uh, size, there should be more. Certainly, more than enough to find the mechanism to operate the hangar door."

"Aye, aye, sir!" Ylon somehow managed to salute in the close confines of the stowage compartment. He donned the mask and squeezed past Blast.

"Sir?" She glanced at Dirk. "Doesn't he know I'm female?"

"Gender specific terms are not used aboard ship," explained Blast. "During the war, my shift was all women. We never used words like Miss, Ma'am or Marm."

Ylon clambered down the side of the skuttle, mask pressed flat against his face to maintain the seal, and bustled to the doors. He examined the wall panel and pressed a button.

The wide circle of hatch narrowed, like the petals of a flower closing. Ylon continued to inspect the controls. He snapped his fingers and then slapped a small section of the panel. His hair fluttered around him, a living halo of golden snakes, as air filled the closed cabin. The clone tore the mask off and motioned for them to join him.

The full blast of the siren hit them as they exited the cabin. Ylon stood with his fingers in his ears, a scowl creasing his features.

"Battle-ready status," shouted Blast, above the blare of horns.

"You mean we're under attack?" Dirk gulped.

"Probably a short in the system," Ylon said.

Finn's daughter glanced despondently about them. "Or us."

"Perhaps we should suit up," said Dirk.

Just then the screeching klaxon fell silent with an exasperated beep.

Gwen tugged at Dirk's sleeve. "Let's get out of here; I don't like feeling so..." her eyes scanned the chamber "... exposed."

"I'm with you." Dirk inclined his head in agreement. He looked at Blast. "Any idea where we're going?"

Ylon answered for his counterpart. "The engine room."

"I know that but where?" said Dirk.

"Well, I only got a glimpse of the line drawings," replied Blast. "I can't remember where the engines would be."

Ylon chuffed. "All ships are basically the same. I

would expect them to be towards the rear of the vessel, so they should be close by."

"Not quite." Blast tilted her head to one side and held up a finger. "The new engines don't have to be in the stern. In the past, timed-jumps were achieved as energy from old propulsion engines was allowed to overload and then discharged," she continued. "I believe the new layout is similar to that of a space station with essential areas located deep within the vehicle for protection."

Dirk turned to Gwen. "We can't go traipsing through the cargo bay. Any handy halls or hidden conduit we can use?"

"I'm sure there are, but..."

Ylon studied the far wall and pointed. "How about taking the exit provided?"

Dirk slapped his forehead. "Why didn't I think of that?"

Gwen muttered in Dirk's ear. "It's amazing that when the time for confrontation came they didn't blast us out of the waters."

"Come on you two," Ylon said. "They could be back any minute."

As if to confirm his statement, there was a soft swoosh marking a change in pressure outside the hangar. Without further ado, the group ducked through the door and into a small hall.

By this time of day the Pennines Bathosphere was a

beehive of activity, with business, such that there was of it, in full swing. For many of the newly unemployed, it was a time for huddling around 3D-vids and watching the game shows and tripe that had replaced the regular Galactic Conflict news updates. That was if they were lucky enough still to have 3D-vid capabilities. Many could no longer afford the luxury, and these people hit the streets to loiter outside shops with large holographic displays and watch their favourite broadcasts. Others prowled restlessly amongst the crowd. Some of them actually looked for work. In any case, they clogged the arteries of the dome like human cholesterol.

The more fortunate had some sort of occupation, no matter how menial, the human having supplanted the inhuman drone in many tasks. The maintenance crew slogged around apathetically, sweeping up here and there, picking up this bit or that, and generally adding to the chaos of congestion.

In other words, it was a day like any other day in the newly recreated post-war world of the complex. A day of sullen resentment and smouldering anger. With tempers ready to flare at the slightest stimulus or inconvenience.

Yet humanity's instinct for survival was such that they never lost hope. For man could recall that their race had survived two World Wars, the melting of the polar ice-caps, the Great Flood and the Exodus. Even three hundred years of Galactic Conflict. They had endured before, surely they would weather this crisis too?

One other thing humanity had in its favour was humour – the need for comic relief to release them from the gloom that surrounded them in the half-light of the geodesic dome. So they weren't quite sure how to react when the agrav system ran amok. As the temperature of the metals wavered from absolute zero, the magnetic field of the superconductors warped. The balance between positive and negative polarities that kept the many conveyance vehicles skimming across the surface was interrupted, developing repellent qualities.

The agrav belt began to spit trucks and carts aloft – sending them caroming off the ceiling, crashing into far walls, or careening out over the pedo-belt. Depending, of course, upon the skill of the human operator. Assuming the conveyance had a driver. The purely automated vehicles went straight up in an uncontrolled ascent to smash into the nearest obstacle, ceiling, roof or – in some cases – next level.

At first, people laughed at a sight so incongruous as the stolid box-cars tossed about like children's toys. It *was* funny. They laughed at trucks bouncing around like ping-pong balls. They laughed at the terrified expression of the drivers as they whizzed overhead. Many hadn't laughed this hard since the old days. The war days when times were good.

Strangers leaned against their nearest neighbours,

clutching on to each other for support. Others clenched bellies taut with gut-wrenching guffaws. Only a few saw the danger.

Until one of the unmanned trucks struck the clear bubble of the dome. *Splat!*

It hit with a deep boom, a rumbling thunder of sound, under which echoed a disconcertingly sharp clack. A few imagined that they saw the dome buckle, bowing outward from the pressure of the blow. Others would have sworn they detected a fissure develop in the plastiglas skin.

Collectively, they held their breath. Laughter froze in their throats; their mouths gone suddenly dry as their eyes grew round and wide. Their jaws unhinged, and they uttered a unified gasp as they waited for the vast superstructure to rupture and for the sea to come spilling in.

Nothing happened. Overhead the dome remained intact and dry, unbreached. Man, woman and child alike exhaled with a huge susurration of air.

Ping ... zing ...

Then old Newtonian laws asserted themselves, and objects – that must travel in a straight line until acted upon by an opposing force – found that force, gravity, and what went up came crashing back down again. And the many trucks and lorries, having completed their ascents, dropped abruptly.

Those below scattered as people were released from their thrall. Bedlam rippled outwards as the terrified citizens ran to get out of the way, for the cars didn't settle tidily around them, but continued to hop and bounce with some sort of ricochet effect. The exodus rapidly turned into a stampede as people elbowed their way up the pedo-belt. Others escaped by taking any available route, clambering over the handrails and any person who happened to be in their path. The confused headed against the normal flow of traffic, swimming like fish upstream. The circumspect dropped where they stood, thinking it was best to expose as little of their anatomy as possible to darting projectiles.

Most of them were trampled underfoot.

The all important retractable shelf was in place. Robbie/AWS was involved in rewiring its interior, attaching the peripheral cords and the hook-ups that would link the computer directly to the servo-mech and permit AWS to access that part of the robot which was its brain.

Soon the monitor and keyboard would be mounted and AWS could begin to download itself into the virgin system. AWS delayed long enough to count the recently completed back-up diskettes and add the sum of those to today's standard back-up. A simple enough procedure to subtract this figure against the expected total to get the number that still needed to be done. Or it should have been.

But AWS lost count. The words to the creator's song got garbled.

"Happy ... happy... Happy days are here again. The skies above are clear do-day. Oh, doo-de-dah-de-doo."

Robbie's claw-like arms trembled. Its visual receptors rolled in their sockets, and the servo-mech peered in mild surprise at the master computer. Solder dribbled, with a thick plop, barely missing the floor of the cabinet, and AWS whistled an imperative at the servo-mech. The robot eyed the splotched carpet and was torn between its primary function of keeping a neat house and the computer's overriding demands.

The servo-mechanism sank on its shock absorbers, releasing the cushioned air through rubber connectors.

PBBBBBTS!

The computer squawked, but Robbie refused to budge until AWS apologized.

Blast and Ylon led them unerringly towards the middle of the ship, using some inborn instinct which told them where the gravitational centre should be.

The halls were nearly deserted, for the searchers had been recalled and were making their way back to the cargo bay for the end of shift. Alerted by the heavy tread of boots, Ylon, Blast, Dirk and Gwen quickly shrank into the background until they passed.

In a relatively short time, the party stood outside the engine rooms staring at the door to end all doors. It was huge, spanning the entire height of the ship. Its surface was plastered with every warning label known to man. Dizzying in the jarring array of colours, Dirk noted the age-old symbols for radiation, explosive, caustics and corrosives, and there were many he did not recognize. He pondered one at eye-level. A simple black and white affair. An hourglass with an X drawn through it.

Ylon walked up beside him. "Time warp."

"You're kidding."

The clone shook his head.

"It's blurred." Dirk squinted. There were two hour-glasses and two Xs almost, but not quite, super-imposed over each other. The effect was disorienting.

"That's what it looks like."

"What?"

"The Doppleganger effect." Ylon swallowed. "One of the less pleasant aspects of the timed-leap. There's blurring and double-vision, and motion leaves trailers or afterimages in the brain."

"Oh."

Gwen stalked from one side of the door to the other, counting the steps. "How'd you find this place so fast?" she said.

"No real problem, going on the assumption that Blast was right and the engines were amidship. It's easy finding centre. It's like having sea legs."

"An old nautical term," explained Blast.

"Yes, I know," said Dirk, "describing how a sailor adjusts his posture to withstand the pitch and roll of the waves, but this is space."

"It has more to do with sense of balance and still translates well in modern times, if you think of balance in terms of how well one adapts to one's environment. In this case a three-dimensional environment." Ylon leered benignly at the humans. "It's something you land-bound people lack, but when you are born in space, you always have a sense of which way's up, which way's down, which way's in and which way's out, even when those terms become relative."

"Unfortunately, it's a sense we lose when we go down to the Earth's surface." Blast chuckled. "If I got a credit for every time I went astray in the stationary bathosphere, I could probably buy this ship."

Dirk folded his hands across his chest. "So, how do we get in?"

Glen glowered at the ident-pad. "Pre-programmed print."

"Great, that's as far as we go then." Dirk turned from the door to stare at the plate. "If we could find a terminal, maybe we could link up with AWS and reprogram the mainframe to take our prints."

"I haven't seen many terminals," said Ylon. "That's odd. They're usually sprinkled throughout a ship. How do they expect to communicate with the air traffic control computers or with AWS?"

"This is a Deep-Space Vehicle," said Gwen. "Perhaps they don't expect it to be able to communicate with AWS?"

"Still with retrievable satellite swarms, AWS's range is good to Charon and conceivably beyond. Although no one's ever gone that far before," added Dirk.

Ylon persisted. "All ships are designed to take instructions from AWS. In a combat situation, the computer can fly a vessel better than any human crew."

"Only because the computer, who took over control of both ships, already knew what the other vessel was going to do," Blast reminded her partner.

"AWS aside," Ylon said, "it's still strange. I mean, how does the captain plan to access the ship's internal system?"

"Voice mode?" Blast suggested.

The clones groaned. "Then we're stuck."

There was a heavy thunk, click and a whir, and they gaped at the spinning wheel of the locking mechanism as it reversed direction.

They dashed away from the door and stopped. There was nowhere to go.

The wheel reversed direction again.

Blast spied a small alcove, grabbed Gwen and steered her towards it. Ylon seized Dirk, and he too

124

was propelled towards the recess. Then they were unceremoniously shoved, face-to-face, nose-to-nose, into a crawlspace so tight that Dirk could hardly breathe.

The clones vanished.

The whirring continued and Dirk's gaze was drawn back to the door. It swung ... and swung ... and swung ... and swung on mammoth hinges. The door was nearly two metres thick. The only other door he had ever seen of comparable size was the main entrances to DSHQ, which had been built to survive a direct nuclear hit.

Muffled voices penetrated their hidden lair.

"How do I know what the alarm was for?" one grumbled. "Nobody's in there now, that's for sure."

Suited individuals materialized briefly, their ghostly forms quickly obscured by the adjoining wall as they headed down the hall, still complaining.

"That's brass for you."

Dirk managed to extricate an arm from between them and mimed walking with index and middle finger. He jerked his thumb towards the door.

Gwen watched the hand and then nodded. Blast's face appeared at the opening, and Dirk hissed in alarm. A tiny hand covered his lips. Dirk was jostled from behind as Gwen began the difficult task of untangling limb from limb.

"I think we're OK," Blast said. Ylon clasped Dirk's wrists and yanked him from the hole while Blast assisted Gwen. Dirk and Gwen exchanged startled glances and then dusted themselves off. The Lilliputian warriors were stronger than their human counterparts too.

They inched towards the entrance. Ylon made a slicing gesture, and they stopped while Blast crept forward to peer around the corner.

She backed out and whispered. "It's clear. It would appear that everyone is gone."

"And they left the engine room unguarded? My father would be horrified." Gwen eyed the door.

"Maybe it'll close automatically."

Dirk looked warily up the hall. "Or ... they're coming back."

"That cuts it," said Ylon. "Do you want to take a look at those engines, or don't you?"

He strode through the open door and dropped into a defensive crouch, reaching for weapons that he, now placed on inactive service, did not possess.

Dirk lifted a shoulder in an ambiguous gesture and followed. Then awe overwhelmed all other emotions. The youth look up ... and up ... and up. Like the door, the engines vaulted to the top of the ship.

"By the sun, moon and stars!" Ylon climbed to his feet. "Look at the size of the thing."

Dirk felt his legs go limp. Until this moment he hadn't believed it, but one glance at the engines and he knew. It was true, all true. Man could achieve the stars.

126

"Who was it that said, 'Give me the lever of the right size and I can move the world'?" he said.

"I don't know," said Gwen. "But it certainly looks like someone set about to prove the theory."

"Well, they've done it, if they've created an engine that can warp time and space," asserted Blast.

At this moment, Dirk stood on a ship capable of . . . of . . . his mind went blank. The possibilities were as immense as the engines. No matter what had happened mankind was free at last.

The door behind them started to move. Ylon shouted, closing the gap between himself and the portal with a single leap.

On the opposite side of the door there was an answering bellow of consternation as their presence inside the chamber was detected. A hand appeared in the aperture and then retreated quickly before it was severed at the wrist.

The massive door shuddered shut, and they were locked in!

17/5/2334

THIRTEEN-HUNDRED HOURS

Pushing Ylon away from the door, Gwen grappled with the wheel. It spun uselessly in her hands. She leaned against it, trying to stop the spin. "My dad's gonna kill me."

She blanched at her choice of words, and the blackened face of the systems analyst rose in her mind's eye. She pushed the image away.

"We'll get out," said Dirk. "There's got to be some other way out."

A sudden clatter behind them diverted their attention away from the door. Dirk and Gwen whirled and all other considerations were arrested by the sight of Ylon and Blast crawling, spider-like, over the wire-mesh engine housing, their faces jammed flat against the lattice-work.

"Will you look at this?" Blast exclaimed. The Lilliputian clone looped her skirts between her legs and wrapped them around her waist to facilitate climbing. Ylon stopped to scrutinize a part of the mechanism, and she passed him, moving higher up the stout metal structure.

Dirk scowled. "What are you two doing?"

Ylon stared at Dirk, bewildered. "Studying the engines, of course. It *is* what we came here for, isn't it?"

"Well, yes, but the situation has changed slightly." He motioned at the door.

"Oh, that." The clone shrugged.

"The capacitor and the conductor coils are mammoth," Blast observed. "Yes, yes, I see how it might work."

Ylon joined Blast, and they clung to the cage like bats. He shook his head. "I bet this baby can go."

Dirk was cautious in spite of himself. "You mean, it'll work?"

"It should," said Blast.

"How?"

"Are you familiar with the concept of linear accelerators? Large devices that generate high frequency pulses used to excite subatomic particles to near light speeds?"

"Yes, but those are antique," protested Dirk. He thought for a moment. "And don't they require some kind of external propulsion mechanism or launch?"

"Yes, that was always a drawback with a viable star drive system. Let's face it, a ship will not always have an external catapult, particularly if it's already in space, and..."

Ylon finished Blast's sentence for her, "... we have one big particle here to accelerate." He grinned.

"You mean, the size of the particle – in this case the ship – regulates the size of the engine needed to drive it?"

"Actually, I'd say the reverse is true," Blast mused out loud. "The size of the engine dictates the size of the particle which can be accelerated. But essentially, you are correct."

"So it's big," said Dirk. "I still don't understand. You just said the concept doesn't work, not out in space."

"We didn't say the theory doesn't work, only the technology. The principle remains the same. To provide enough impetus to drive an object beyond the speed of light," Ylon said.

Blast laid a hand on his shoulder. "Maybe it would help if we explained the theory to him. Star drive, or the timed-leap function as we now have it, is a strange mixture of the two displacement theories – both electrical and aerodynamic. If you think electrical, then consider the amount of current required to produce movement across a medium, say a copper wire. As you know, a proportional increase in flux ratio is needed to propel the charge across the void of space."

"Yes," said Dirk.

"Our timed-jumps utilize this principle, although the capability was discovered quite by accident in our own engines. The current coil provides enough flux to displace the mass – the vessel – assuming, of course, that the mass is lighter than air that surrounds it. That's aerodynamics."

"Huh?"

"Yes, the whole theory does sort of get fuzzy around the edges when you consider the size of the ship. You'll just have to trust me on this. The former linear accelerator has been internalized, acting on itself and the item that surrounds it."

Dirk turned to the object of their quest. "So this is star drive."

"Yes, it looks like it, and it's a beauty," replied Blast. "I only got a glimpse of the schematics. I wish I could explain it better, but I'm not that much of a technician."

Dirk contemplated her earlier comments and chuckled. "Never would have guessed."

Ylon fiddled with his moustache. "I can see now why they couldn't convert the *Revenant.* While our ships are smaller, not needing an engine of this magnitude, still, they would have to knock out most of the living quarters to make enough room, leaving the *Revenant* with a skeleton crew."

Behind them, the door began to ring metallically. *Clang. Crack!*

Dirk jumped.

"Great," he hissed, "we've got company."

Clack. Bang!

"We need to get out of here," said Dirk to Gwen, out of the corner of his mouth.

She looped her arms across her chest. "How do you suggest we do that?"

"I don't know. I thought you might have some ideas. It's your ship after all." He swung back to Ylon and Blast but they had clambered over the top of the cage and were hidden behind the bulk of the engines.

Bang. Crash!

"Well, I haven't a clue, or I'd've left by now," she said.

"Why *are* they knocking?" said the exasperated Dirk. "They have the key; we don't. It's not as if we could let them in."

"I wouldn't recommend it," quipped Gwen.

"In answer to your first question, Dirk," Ylon said, as he strolled around the side of the metal cage, "I can imagine that whoever's beyond the door isn't horribly bright, and no, I don't suppose they have the code, or they would have used it. They're probably waiting for someone who does."

"There must be an auxiliary exit," said Dirk.

"No," Blast said, as she popped into view.

"No?" The youth's voice cracked. "There must be."

"We could look for one," Blast climbed down from her perch, "but I doubt if you'll find it."

"I don't believe it," stated Dirk, emphatically. "This is an engine room; accessibility is vital. They have to be able to get in and out to make repairs."

The racket continued. Dirk winced, stuck his finger in his ear and twiddled it around.

"Normally this room would be manned at all times," Ylon asserted. "But there's a more important purpose for the room, and that's containment. The area must be sealed off immediately in the event of an accident. You saw the thickness of the door. It's built to withstand explosion, implosion, proton and neutron radiation, any form of leakage that could harm passengers and crew."

"There's got to be another exit," Dirk insisted flatly.

"I suppose when you think about it, that might qualify." Ylon crooked a thumb at the ceiling some thirty metres above their heads.

"Huh? What?" Dirk squinted at the jumble of pipes and ventilator shafts.

"There." Ylon pointed again. "The emergency outlet valve that acts as a vent or a chimney into space in case containment is breached. It's the only violation of an engine room's overall tensile structure allowed according to military specifications."

The banging stopped.

"So we can get out."

"It's not what I'd call a particularly hospitable environment outside," said Gwen.

"What about suits?"

"Unlikely that you'll find them in here," said Blast. "They'd be outside."

"What? Hanging on the side of the ship?" Dirk yelped.

"No, somewhere else in the ship."

He shook his head. "Come now, what about emergencies? Some provision must be made for the engineering crew."

"The only use for suits would be to provide protection during clean up after an incident," said Ylon.

"What about escape?" Dirk shot an oblique glance at Gwen for reassurance that he was correct. She examined the tops of her shoes.

"Escape? From what?" said Ylon. "If the engines go, you wouldn't survive. You wouldn't want to."

"Can we reach the vent?"

"There's probably a catwalk tucked into one of the walls, but I wouldn't bother if I were you."

"Why not?"

"Like I said, the purpose of the engine room, besides housing the engine, is containment. The ventilation cap is not meant to open except under extreme pressures. The hatch is probably sealed and voice-activated, like the door. Without our prints on the security records, without the code, we couldn't possibly budge it."

The Lilliputian clone held out a hand. "And before you ask, no. We couldn't jemmy it or pry it open. Considering the size of the engines, I'd say there's probably several tons of some lead-reinforced metal alloy weighing down the lid."

"Great! We're trapped."

"That's about the size of it."

Dirk persisted: "So what do we do now?"

Blast knelt on the floor, wrapping her skirts about her feet. "Wait, I suppose. Somebody's bound to come with the right code eventually. Until then," she produced a stylus and paper from the folds of her gown, "I'm going to make a drawing of the beast."

Dirk squatted next to his friends. "Why? Without the schematics and line drawings of the inner mechanism, it's of little use."

Blast made a face. "It's better than nothing."

"What do you mean, nothing? The information is still on computer."

Ylon's gaze followed Gwen's agitated pacing around the room. "If her father's in on this, can you be sure of that now that we've alerted him?"

Dirk ducked his head in assent. "I see what you mean." Then putting the best face on it, he gestured broadly and said: "No problem, we've got the working model."

"Don't you mean it has got us?"

*   *   *

The intruders were inside the engine room!

The apprentice-technician yanked his arm from the door just before his hand would have been severed at the wrist. His supervisor was long gone. The man swore. He was a lowly apprentice, and he didn't have the clearance to get into the engine room unescorted. He eyed the door. It needed a grade-two technician, at least, to activate this thing. He raced off to find his superior.

When he next returned, it was with a balky and reluctant grade three in tow.

"Why do these things always have to happen at the end of shift?" the technician complained bitterly as he clumped along in his unwieldy boots.

"Please, sir, just stand guard until I can bring the supervisor."

"Why? The people inside aren't going anywhere."

"Look, if they manage to get out," the apprentice gesticulated excitedly, "do you want to explain it to security? I most certainly don't."

Both men stopped to consider the steely-eyed Marks.

"OK, kid, go find the foreman."

The young man dashed away. Angry, the technician kicked at the portal.

Clang!

"And I had plans for tonight." He kicked it again.

Crack!

He picked up a spanner and began banging on the metal surface.

Bang ... bang ... bang ...

Someone somewhere shouted.

Bang ... bang ... bang ...

More yells and cries echoed in the background in answer to his insistent pounding.

The supervisor sprinted around the corner. "What in heaven's name do you think you're doing?"

The technician gave the door a half-hearted swipe with the spanner before retorting, "I didn't even dent it."

"Yes, but why are you trying?"

"They're in there."

"What! Who?"

"The intruders. They're in there. The apprentice saw them when I sent him back to make sure the security lock had engaged."

"Well, you can stop hitting the door. It won't help."

"Makes me feel better..."

"Pardon?"

"Oh, nothing," he grumbled.

The supervisor studied the door. "They're not going any place, and you're sure not going to get in that way."

The technician shouldered his spanner. "Get in? Who me? Who wants to get in? I don't have the clearance, remember. You've got the code. You go in if you want to. I don't. They might be armed."

"Then why are you –" The foreman studied the technician. "Oh, never mind. I'll go and report this to the central station. I'm pretty sure that they'll want to send security over. You stay put!"

"Sure." The technician dropped the spanner with a crash. "I'll guard the door."

"Watch what you're doing! We're supposed to be building this ship, not destroying it."

The technician grunted, dug around in his pocket for a cigarette and slouched against the wall.

"Make sure they don't get out."

"Get out, right. Like they're gonna fly."

"They got in, didn't they? How do you know that they don't have access to the computer?"

The technician picked up the spanner again and cradled it.

The foreman glowered at the tool. "And don't break anything."

The technician gave him a wide-eyed innocent look. "Who me? I wouldn't dream of it."

Dirk slumped against a panel, checking first to ensure he would not touch any buttons or toggle any unknown switches with his action. Gwen continued to prowl around the room, her anxiety mounting.

Their situation looked bleak, and he cursed himself for not going through the proper channels, despite the delays. If he had, they would all be safe and snug at home. Dirk stared at the engines and reviewed his options.

There had to be something he could do. He glanced at the door which had become disconcertingly silent. Given a laser torch and a few hours, maybe, he could cut his way through, but he had neither.

The vent? His gaze drifted to the complicated mass of pipe and wire above his head, and he dismissed the idea.

Ylon wandered to the opposite side of the room and stopped next to Gwen to explain the purpose of some miscellaneous part, or other. Not far away, Blast leaned over pen and pad intent on her drawing. Dirk grinned as he noticed her tongue sticking from the corner of her mouth.

The warrior clone's words drifted across the chamber. "... of course, it's a computer function ..."

Computers! Of course! He threw up his hands. Why hadn't he thought of that? Dirk levered himself away from the panel. He might as well try to do something productive.

The youth eyed the chamber, still baffled by what he saw, or more importantly, didn't see. There had to be a terminal in here. Somewhere. Something to orchestrate all the gadgets and gizmos. He made a rude noise. It made no sense. Surely they needed access to the ship's computers to make course adjustments, internal modifications, or complete software restorations. Yet he could see nothing that might allow him to communicate with the mainframe besides the occasional microphone pick-ups. Neither keyboard nor keypad upon which he could spell out complex commands.

Course adjustments would be bridge controlled. But even assuming this was a peacetime vessel and not subject to attack, there was always the possibility that the bridge could be knocked out – by collision with a meteorite or an asteroid, for instance. A contingency system had to be set up elsewhere on the vessel, and this was the most logical place, seeing how it was built to withstand both impact or explosion.

Perhaps Ylon was right; the computer was solely voice-activated.

Dirk scratched his head. Something about the concept grated. From a security standpoint, voice-activated computers had obvious weaknesses. Just as computer hardware had advanced through the war years so had the science of espionage. And what was spoken could be overheard. While Dirk knew that he was unusual in favouring keyboards over verbal commands, he preferred them for an obvious reason, and that was privacy. With the kind of paranoia he had seen around here, Dirk couldn't believe that the ship had no manual interface.

No, the youth decided, there had to be a keyboard concealed around here somewhere.

If he could get to the on-board computers...

Dirk's hands trembled at the thought of digging around in the guts of this mechanized monster. One false move and he could blast them to kingdom come.

His fingers began a microscopic examination. Gingerly the youth tapped the metal facing, listening for a hollow sound that might signify a cavity in which a small terminal might be secreted.

And as he did, he prayed that he wouldn't trip a switch that would send them rocketing off to the next galaxy.

"We've got 'em," said Marks to Finn where he sat, bent and puzzling over the schematics.

The commander glanced up from the holo display and said: "Huh?"

Marks clarified. "The kids."

Finn straightened, the vertebrae crackling into alignment. With a last harried glimpse at the floating graphics, he switched off the projection table to concentrate on his security chief. He did not like the gloating tone of the man's voice. "Well, where are they?"

"Just where you expected them to be: the big ship."

"Foolish girl." Finn clicked his tongue in disapproval. "How far did they get?"

"To the engine room."

"You mean . . ."

Their eyes locked, and Finn's face whitened from its normally robust hue as he saw the look in Marks's eyes, and Finn knew what the other man was thinking.

Their visitors could not be permitted to leave, not now, not with this information. They were so close to completion.

If it had just been young Alexander and his friends, maybe they'd've been able to tough it out. The ship was operational and they could always move it. The *Manta*'s virgin flight had been carefully planned, timed to coincide with the destruction of all available data from AWS and final patent approval. All official logs and entry tapes here had been purged of their visit. Pulling a few strings, even the shuttle crew could be persuaded to forget their arrival. It could be made to appear that they never had been here. Without proof and back-up, who would believe them?

But his daughter had become involved. She could provide eye-witness testimony, not only to their presence, capture and detainment within the space station, but confirmation of the existence of the ship.

If the young Alexander and his clone friends returned to Earth, and Finn's daughter accompanied them, the theft would be revealed for what it was and the secret would be out. All the technical data that he had so carefully purloined and then expunged from AWS would be disclosed, and the new *Manta* would, in due course of time, be declared public domain.

The security director pivoted and faced his commander. "There are measures we can take to ensure that no one escapes from the engine room. They are caught in a chamber with any number of controlled substances. Flooding the area would be easy."

"My daughter's in there!" Finn cried, and then tried to ignore Marks's expression. It wasn't difficult to guess what was on the man's mind.

"They're trespassing in a high security area, and it would provide an immediate and quick fix," said Marks briskly. "After all, the kid's not supposed to be here anyway. And no one will miss the clones. Accidents do happen."

"You must be crazy if you think I'll consent to that!"

Marks's eyes turned into brittle pinpricks of light. "Crazy? Must I remind you that you are responsible for everything that transpires within this facility. Everything. Even if you could deny knowledge of any irregularities, you will still be held accountable." He flicked nonchalantly at a bit of dust upon his epaulettes.

Finn fumed. No reply he could think of was sufficient. The man must be mad.

"All right," Marks conceded, "if you don't want to take action, then why don't I go and collect your daughter? We can decide what to do with the rest of them later."

Finn stuttered, reluctant to put Gwen in Marks's custody. "There's, ah, no real rush. They're secure. Let my daughter cool her heels inside the engine room. Give her a chance to think about childish rebellion. In a little while, we can separate her from the rest. I'll give her a stern talking to; she can contemplate the consequences of her actions."

The security director stared disdainfully down upon Finn.

"You can't stall for ever, sir," he said, with typical mock servility. "A decision must be made."

Finn sprang to his feet and roared. "Yes, I know, but not now ... not now."

Gwen checked her watch for something like the tenth time in the last five minutes. Fear had been replaced by tedium and then by boredom.

Ylon and Blast sat Indian style on the floor, making minute corrections, identifying parts and labelling them.

"I don't believe it," Gwen fumed. "We've been here for hours."

"Not quite," said Ylon. "One-point-four-two hours to be precise."

She strode over to Dirk, who was busily prising

another dark green panel from the wall and put her hands on her hips.

"It would be just like my father to give me time to think of 'the error of my ways'."

The panel he was working on snapped back into place, pinching his fingers. He stuck them inside his mouth and swore around them. "Mmmrph."

She peered quizzically at the youth. "Are you sure there's no mistake? This has always been treated like a top secret project. Are you sure the Council didn't OK this and not, uh, bother to consult you about it?"

"I'm your father's direct superior," he snarled irritably. "I'm head of DSHQ, nominally at least. Anything to do with deep-space exploration has to go through me."

She eyed him. "You're awfully young, though."

"Yeah, don't I know it. My father never tires of reminding me."

"Mine too." Gwen gazed desolately at the floor.

"I think that's part of the job description."

She cocked her head, perplexed.

"Of being a father." He attacked the panel again. "Reminding kids that they're young."

She nodded in terse agreement. "What are you doing?"

"Trying to find a keyboard. Why else should I subject myself to this torture?" He examined his fingers.

"I don't know. You're a frustrated engineer and

your parents never gave you an erector set when you were a kid," she retorted.

"No, the way I figure it, there's got to be a keyboard somewhere. Something for communiqués that you wouldn't want overheard," Dirk said. "If I can get through to AWS, maybe I can get us out of here. Crack the code, get the on-boards to accept our voice prints, handprints ... something."

"Oh, why didn't you say so? I can help." She pulled a nail file from a pocket.

"You meant to say you've had that all this time!"

"Sorry, I didn't know what you were doing." Gwen gave a shake of her thick, red hair and began to gouge at a panel with the file.

"I've already checked that one." He motioned with a jerk of his head to his opposite side. "That's the direction I'm going."

She switched sides and went back to the previous topic. "You said yourself that you're *nominal*," she stressed the word, "head of DSHQ. Nominal, correct me if I'm wrong, but that means in name only."

She noticed the peevish expression that crossed his face and considered her next words carefully. "You were placed in charge mainly because at the very beginning you were the only human who could interface with the computer."

"Well, yes, I suppose that's true."

"And interfacing with AWS would be your primary

function? So maybe –" she stopped digging at the panel and faced him – "the Council forgot."

"Forgot?"

"To tell you. I mean you have more important things to do, like feeding the population, getting the tanker fleet running. Maybe the Council just didn't mention the prototype?"

"My father's a member of the Council. Even if they did decide to start work on a new ship and somehow overlooked me in the normal chain of command, he would have mentioned it. Even though he looks over my shoulder all the time to make sure I don't make any mistakes, he also looks out for my interests."

"Are you sure? Your dad must be a lot more open with you than mine is with me."

"Maybe, although I doubt it." Dirk frowned. "However, that's supposed to be the advantage of the new open system. No secrets." Dirk gave up on the panel. "I can't say it's worked out all that well."

"Don't I know it," said Gwen. "Everything is a lot worse than it was before."

"Thanks, I needed that." Dirk's voice faltered before he went on. "You really think so?"

She let out a short, sharp bark of laughter. "You have to ask?"

"I didn't mean for it to be like this."

"Hey, you can't be responsible for other people's actions. The problem is that people haven't changed. They still want secrets, and they still keep them."

"Thanks, I guess that should help, but it doesn't." He scooted around her to the next panel. "But when you come to think about it, as far as AWS is concerned I have the higher security clearance. Assuming the Council made the decision to build the *Manta* without my being consulted, the system would have known and it would have alerted me, even if my father did not."

He slammed his fist into the panel, hard. An alarm burbled somewhere and Ylon and Blast looked up from their drawings.

Dirk withdrew his hand as if burned. The alarm stilled.

"Careful," remonstrated Blast.

"Sorry," said Dirk. He began to work on the panel again more cautiously. "To think that we could've escaped to the stars long ago, and the military just sat on it."

"Considering the date on the file-specs," said Blast, "they may have been completely justified in suppressing the information. It was during the Exodus, and the mass migration was still on-going. They would have had neither the time nor material to implement such a programme."

"Wouldn't that have been the perfect time?" said Gwen.

"Not practical."

"Impossible," commented Ylon.

"You know," said Dirk, "I thought we'd discovered

something great. I thought people would be pleased. I brought the plans here directly because I didn't want them to get caught up in subcommittees while everyone decided who owned the rights. We need a prototype. We need to find out if it's capable of doing what it's supposed to do before we get people all worked up about it."

Dirk sagged against the leg of a workbench. "I give up. I don't know what to do."

Gwen leaned forward, reaching out in sympathy. She looked at her hand and let it drop into her lap.

Suddenly from somewhere behind them, there came a grinding noise, followed by a thud and a soft whir. The locking wheel began to rotate and spin. First right and then left.

Gwen stiffened and swung towards the door.

The massive portal shuddered, sweeping forward on silent hinges. Sluggishly at first, opening by inches and degrees to reveal each layered thickness of silvered steel.

Then a leg, an arm, a hand, appeared in the widening gap . . .

Half an hour later Gwen found herself back in her room, where she had been unceremoniously bundled by armed guards, presumably sent by her father.

She paced back and forth, rubbing her wrists furiously to get the circulation back into her hands where they'd been cuffed. Frustrated, she slapped at the wall unit, missing the ident-key deliberately, wanting the door to open to her and fearing it would not. For Gwen knew the routine. Her father would keep her grounded until she admitted her mistake, or pretended to.

Absolution would take a while – an eternity in this instance – but she could begin the process and apologize. The idea rankled, but she had Dirk and the

Lilliputian friends to think about. She had to help somehow, although Gwen didn't know how. If she swallowed her pride, her father might let her move about within the station, and helping them would be a lot easier to accomplish if she didn't have her father watching her every minute.

Gwen tested the door. It slid back into the wall. She stared at her palm, surprised that it hadn't been secured against her print and the computer ident fixed into manual override. Then she noted the chair placed in front of her door. A rifle rested against it.

Good grief, she was being guarded. She wondered by whom. The image of steely-eyed Marks surfaced, and she shivered.

Muffled voices drifted to her, coming from her father's office. She slipped closer to the door to listen.

"We're in trouble," Ylon said, as the trio watched the door swing close.

"That fact is just dawning on you, dear?" Blast drawled and winked.

The clone gave a snort of laughter and stuffed his hands in his pockets. "No, but I don't think I realized how much until now."

"True. They do not wish us well." Blast eyed the door. "I'd rather hoped someone would say: 'Oops, so sorry, my mistake.' Or make some excuse." She mimicked Finn's precise military inflection: " 'Ah, yes, those plans. Yes, sir! I misunderstood.' "

Ylon draped a leg over a metal casing. "I would have accepted a simple: 'Aw, shucks, I was going to surprise you.'"

"What are you going on about?" snapped Dirk.

Ylon studied the youth's face and huffed. "You still don't get it, do you?"

The tiny warrior shook his head. "Blast, you explain it to him."

"You don't have to explain it to me," said Dirk. "I know we're in trouble."

"Terminal trouble," amended Ylon.

"Terminal?"

"Yes, terminal, as in lethal."

"You don't mean... You can't..." Dirk's voice dwindled as he digested the unpalatable thought.

Ylon said, "I don't know about Finn; I don't think he's the power behind this, but that man Marks. I don't like the look of him."

"The problem is, Dirk," Blast said, "you've not had the benefit of military training where you learn that human life is expendable. A statistic. A number in a book. We are, from the military perspective, just a couple of digits to add to a report somewhere."

"Certainly, if they had any intention of freeing us, they lost the last opportunity to do so and still save face," Ylon explained. "Until that door closed, they could pretend innocence. They could say they didn't know who was trapped in here. A reasonable enough assertion with a report of intruders in a top secret area. The door shuts automatically. Simple. An accident. No harm done.

"Just as they could have justified their actions by proclaiming that the ship was a personal venture. If Finn turned over the completed craft now, no one would ask what his purpose was in building it or question the clandestine nature of the operation. He could always claim that he chose not to reveal the exact nature of the vessel until he knew it worked."

Dirk nodded. It was the very excuse he'd used for not taking the information to the Council himself.

"Now, though, Finn can't fall back on ignorance or profess innocence. He knows who's imprisoned in here. He knows he's got us caught like three rats in a trap, and he's still keeping us here against our wishes."

An uneasy expression flitted across Dirk's face. "Well, we're not just anybody. We're the liaisons to AWS. Somebody's bound to notice we're missing and they'll start searching."

"Yes, and that fact, which he chooses to ignore, shows a measure of confidence on Finn's part that I personally find disconcerting," said Ylon.

"Are you so sure, Dirk, that they will know where to look?" Blast said. "Way out here at an orbital space station. By your own admission, it's your first trip, an unscheduled one at that, and we didn't tell anyone where we were going."

"AWS knows."

"If anyone thinks to ask."

"The dock workers, the shuttle crew, the security personnel. They've all seen us." Dirk gave a quick duck of his head, as if the assured motion could convince not only himself, but his friends also. "We can be traced."

"You mean," said Ylon, not unkindly, "that nice man, Marks? Humph! Something tells me that that gentleman's veracity is doubtful at best. And the others? The dock workers, the shuttle crew, can be bribed into forgetfulness. Neither group were what you could call friendly."

Blast laughed. "They thought we were nuts, and we weren't on any passenger list that I know of."

Ylon mused out loud. "Bodies are easy enough to dispose of out here in space."

"You've got to be kidding!" said Dirk.

The two simply stared at him.

"You aren't kidding, are you?"

"No, Dirk, we're serious, dead serious."

"But he can't..."

Ylon drove his point home. "You haven't noticed that they're all old military here. I don't know exactly where they came from, but you can tell by their deportment and demeanour. Do you think any of them are going to be put off by killing –" he grimaced distastefully, "– clones? They've been doing it for years. What's another couple, more or less?"

"But I'm –" Dirk stopped himself.

"Human?" Ylon finished his statement for him. "True, that's probably the reason we are all still alive now. They don't quite know what to do with you. That, and I doubt Finn wanted his daughter to witness our demise, but once that obstacle was removed, we become an inconvenience. A regrettable inconvenience, a temporary inconvenience, but an inconvenience nonetheless."

"Great! That's cut it." Dirk sprang to his feet. "We've got to find a link-up to the ship's main computer."

The effect of the wyrme and its self-replicating descendants rippled outward, in ever larger loops. Like a boulder dropped into a placid pond. The errors ranged from the ridiculous, such as the issue of cleated mountain boots for every resident of the underwater facility, to the mildly ominous as important files vanished into a silicon netherworld.

The cumulative impact, though, was perilous. To life and to limb. Of which the temperature flux along the superconductor highway, with its catastrophic results, was only one example.

In some long forgotten dream, AWS dredged up a pre-war macro and followed its instruction, dumping dry chemicals at the hydroponics plant and contaminating the Earth's meagre supply of food. The beleaguered program shut down the air supply to little-used portions of the facility, conserving energy and strength, and toxic wastes normally filtered through the system seeped into the bathosphere.

Yet for the moment, the incidents remained isolated. Distant and far removed from general inspection. A few suffered headaches or a slight distortion of vision.

For the most part, bemused residents pondered unrequested footwear and wondered when they'd next get an opportunity to use it. More than a few had cause to curse their individual terminals. But such an act was trivial in the universal order of things. As often as man worked with computers, who did not have reason to curse them at least once a day when fingers tangled on keyboards or, for reason of pronunciation and syntax, verbal commands were perverted?

Those who were worst off, the survivors of the superconductor fiasco, simply nursed their injuries and hoped to never see the like again. And all remained blissfully oblivious to things transpiring around them.

Then the wyrme crossed the network that bridged AWS with the many civilian systems in the undersea world – scorching the banking net and turning it to cinders. In so doing, it gobbled up the entire fiscal earnings of the mineral filtration plant in New Atlantis. The wyrme belched its metaphoric flame and all the cash assets – or computerized credits, after the manner of the day – of the Robotics Workers Union were deleted.

Repair was one of the few purely human occupations that never boasted a surfeit of labourers, and the RWU was the richest union in existence. The only union still in existence. After all, someone had to keep the machines of the bathosphere operational. Even maintenance droids broke down sometimes.

So when the union's executives saw their bank balance, billions and billions in international credits, slither to the bottom of the screen and vanish, they were not amused. Especially when they tried to recall the number and discovered that neither the balance nor the account existed any more.

Lights on the communications net all over the City and in the government offices blazed as worried businessmen and suicidal stockbrokers called to report their losses.

Impervious to human concerns, the wyrme munched on, entering the computers of the stock exchanges from Tibetan Islands to the Andes chain. And the systems, both monetary and computerized, that held the planetary economy of loosely associated archipelagoes together, crashed.

Dirk's father, George, buried his face in his hands and groaned.

It was like a recurring dream. No, a nightmare, a nightmare he had had since that day six months ago when he had stood among wreckage not unlike that which he witnessed now. Then row upon row of plants, tomatoes, lettuce, chard and cabbage blackened and died on computerized cue.

And it was happening again!

Once green leaves were speckled with the brown-and-yellow of chemical burn as AWS dumped undiluted fertilizer on dry roots.

George took off his spectacles and cleaned them, as though by his action he could erase the view or scrub away the spots still clearly visible upon leaf and stem. He peered myopically around the greenhouse. It didn't help. Even without his spectacles, the leaves still looked brown. Blurry, but brown.

Next to him, a tomato plant drooped and shed its leaves in a rasping shower. George deflated, as if he were carrying the weight of the entire world upon his shoulders.

Rotating slowly on the ball of his foot, George made a full circle, unconsciously mimicking his movements in the previous crisis as he tried to survey and assess the damage dispassionately. Yet his emotions were displayed in the swift contortion of his features. Disbelief and dismay trotted briefly across his face, turning to consternation and disgust. George reached out and touched a plant. It crumbled to dust.

Behind him, George heard the forlorn trickle of water as the precious fluid trapped in the curved pipes found its way out of an open duct.

He noticed the spectacles in his hands and rubbed at them vigorously before reseating them on his nose. The growlights, at their weakest cycle when the sun was at its zenith, flickered and flashed.

George swore.

Then with a heavy sigh, he turned his back on the dying foliage and left the greenhouse to follow the curved plastic pedo-tube down to the next level. George hesitated for a moment, just outside the door to the quonset-style hut where they grew the meat.

He extracted a hankie from his pocket and covered his nose. He paused to take a deep breath before stepping inside to confront the ruined slabs of shri-velled purple beef lying in beds of pseudo-blood.

Even through the cloth, the air stank of spoiled meat. He shifted from foot to foot, trying to hold his breath, until he was forced to inhale. He gagged.

George pinched the bridge of his nose between thumb and forefinger, gasping for air, needing time to think.

The day had begun with such promise. With pre-cious water on its way to the lunar colonies, the Earth could negotiate for the food they so desperately needed. He wondered if something they had done – like so many other times – caused bugs in the system to surface elsewhere.

With fatal results.

Now he regretted giving Dirk the day off. George himself had left DSHQ late. Splitting his time between one facility and another was no easy task with the hydroponics farms located far from the city-complex in another dome-sphere altogether. He had ordered a skimmer, getting to the plant around noon.

Then there'd been the usual preliminaries, petty crises that occurred every time George went to Council meetings. Niggling things that must be corrected immediately, and no one else among his staff seemed to have the wit or the gumption to do it. The farms themselves could have been run without human intervention. In fact, *had* been run without human intervention when George still trusted the computer system. Lately, though, he relied more on human eyes and ears.

Still, it had been late by the time he'd had a chance to tour the greenhouse domes, and the flaws in his reasoning became obvious. First it presumed the said humans knew what they were looking for. Second it presumed they cared.

Somewhere the computer gave an inappropriate command; a valve opened; something spat, spewing blood. And George's specs were sprinkled red.

George yanked the handkerchief from his mouth and plucked the glasses from his nose. The vats of wrinkled meat faded into a blue-black blur. He swished droplets around on the glass, smearing them. He brushed his hair away from his face, leaving a scarlet trail across his forehead.

Then he returned his attention to his specs, spitting on them.

Another valve opened. Something burbled, and George ceased his agitated polishing. Pretty soon there wouldn't be any lens left. With a calm he did not feel, George Alexander slid the earpieces over his ear and shoved the glasses up to the bridge of his nose.

Ignoring the wreckage around him, he walked stiffly over to a terminal and stared in dismay at the display. A warning light blinked steadily. He counted the beats per minute.

His legs gave out from underneath him and the Food Minister collapsed into a chair. If he'd relied on the computer, checking with it when he'd first come in, instead of upon people, it might have told him that something was amiss.

He couldn't handle it. Not again. There were no reserves, no handy supply of irradiated food dating back to pre-flood days. No back-up whatsoever.

"No," he said, a whispered entreaty, a prayer. More chemicals fell into the tubs with a dry rasp.

The computers, the blasted computers. He spun back to face the VDU and began tapping on the keyboard.

He'd hired people to be his eyes and ears, but it was the computers that were supposed to test each trough, check the chemical composition of the liquid mixture and then regulate the flow of water versus fertilizer.

Where had the computer been during all this? Asleep? If it had noticed the error, why hadn't it stopped it?

He finished the final digit of his password and bashed enter. The terminal beeped in protest, churned a bit and then faltered.

`CODE NOT RECOGNIZED. ACCESS DENIED.`

"What!" he roared. "AWS, where are you when I need you?" He keyed in the call number for Dirk's terminal.

And swore when the words — `NO ANSWER AT THAT EXTENSION, WOULD YOU LIKE TO TRY ANOTHER NUMBER?` — appeared on the screen.

Where, for that matter, was his son? Or Dirk's Lilliputian friends?

He folded his arms across the keyboard and rested his head on his forearms. On the screen the letters exploded and fell like glowing rain.

AWS stepped back to survey its work, or more precisely, Robbie went into reverse so that the computer could get a better view of the modifications.

"Happy days are here again. The skies, the skies above are clear again so let's sing … sing … sing … hic." AWS's nearly human voice disintegrated to a mechanical gargle.

162

Robbie cast a sidelong look at the terminal from one of its many new eyes.

"Happy days..."

AWS assessed its work. The monitor and keyboard were wired into place. The speakers and voder box were connected. The eyes ... the eyes ... the megabrain stumbled on the word ... the visual receptors were now positioned on all four sides of the box. A few more improvements and it would be time to finish the transfer ... the transfer of... AWS drew a blank.

With a snap of micro fingers, it remembered ... of data and information files, of course.

Robbie dropped slightly on its hinged supports. A soft breath of air was expelled, sounding like a human gasp, and the servo-mech inserted another back-up disk in the drive in its belly and hit Enter, continuing the process that AWS forgot, lost in another loop of imagination.

"Happy days are here again. The skies, the skies above are ... uh ... uh ... hic."

The youth headed for the next wall panel.

"Dirk," said Ylon. "You're going about it the wrong way."

"Now he tells me."

Ylon winced. "A terminal wouldn't be secreted in a wall. Totally useless if you want to type with any speed and proficiency. What you should be looking for is a table or desk-type set up."

"They're locked."

"Well, there perhaps we can be of help." Blast stepped up beside Ylon and nodded at the regulation tool kit that hung around his waist. "Whatever's been locked," she said brightly, "can always be unlocked again."

Ylon bent to fiddle with the mechanism on the nearest drawer.

Dirk lowered himself to the floor.

"Sorry." The clone glanced up at him. "I haven't been much practical help. Until . . ." He indicated the door with a wave of his hand. "I didn't see the need as long as Gwen was with us. We've lost that edge, and I'm ashamed to admit I underestimated our adversary."

The Lilliputian clone wriggled the tiny Allen wrench in the slot. *Click!*

Ylon sat back, resting on his haunches. "There. Educated guess tells me that this is the most likely spot for them to put a terminal, if they're going to have one. Let's see if my surmise is correct."

He pulled the drawer open. Hands against Ylon's shoulders, Blast peered into the drawer and clapped her partner on the back. "Success!"

Ylon gave Dirk a sheepish grin.

The youth unfolded from the floor and took his place upon the chair. "I'm glad you found it before I dismantled this entire engine room and tripped something that sent us and the entire space station to Alpha Centauri.''

Gwen pressed against the wall as she listened to her father, Marks and the absent guard.

"Have you erased the enquiries, the security tapes and holos of their arrival?" asked Finn.

"As soon as they left the shuttle port," said the guard.

"And what do you propose to do with our unexpected visitors, sir?" Marks asked as he leaned against the desk.

The girl grimaced, noticing how Marks fell back on the courtesy of rank when he was going to propose something particularly odious.

"I don't know. I just don't know," said Finn.

"We could flood the engine room with radiation," suggested Marks.

"No, no, that won't do," said Finn. "There are the bodies to think of and the decontamination of the ship so near completion to think of. And no guarantee that some satellite or ship won't pick up the alarm and relay it back to Earth."

"Perhaps we could take our guests for a little ride?"

Silence. Gwen looked around the door frame as Finn's jaw dropped.

"We must do something," Marks said ominously. "We can't just let them report back to Earth."

"I know," Finn mumbled. "What about my daughter?"

Marks deferred comment.

Finn sighed. "Someday, I hope, she'll understand, but for now we'd better keep her under lock and key for her own protection. I'd say you'd better get back to your post," he said, addressing the guard. Gwen retreated into the shadows.

"What about our friends?"

"Lose them," Finn growled.

Marks chortled unpleasantly. "How, sir?" He leered at the commander.

"I don't care how. I don't want to know about the details. Just do it."

Marks bowed and saluted. "With your permission, sir, I will leave you now to make preparations."

17/5/2334

FIFTEEN-HUNDRED HOURS

"OK, now we should be able to get somewhere," Dirk said. He cracked his knuckles and stared at the prompt. MRSVAX: LOG ON:

He stretched and wriggled his fingers and prepared to type.

After the prompt he added: LINK TO DSHQVAX.

LOG ON: the computer replied implacably.

He pursed his lips, stymied. Dirk had hoped since he was only requesting intermediate interface with another system that he could circumvent such formalities. He tried again.

LOG ON: the computer repeated insistently.

What name would the ship's computer recognize without question?

As part of DSHQ and Finn's direct superior, Dirk's

name should be in the database somewhere, either in the personnel directory or as a part of the organizational charts. Assuming the system formed a direct link to AWS, his name and password *should* be acknowledged.

However, if Finn were smart, he would have tagged Dirk's name to prevent just such an incursion into the space station's computers. That's what Dirk would have done if their situations had been reversed. And Dirk had no reason to believe that Finn was stupid. Use of his own name would alert the commander the minute Dirk signed on.

No, he couldn't risk it.

MRVSVAX: LOG ON: The words reappeared on another line and blinked at him. The two clones watched him, sensing his quandary.

The youth snapped his fingers. "I know."

F-I-N-N

PASSWORD:

Oh, oh, Dirk had been through this before. He didn't have time for a quick jaunt through the dictionary while he tried to figure out what the password might be. When in doubt – guess. He typed the first thing that came to mind.

GWEN

FINN, PERRY, the computer responded. CURRENTLY LOGGED ON TERMINAL 1203 IN THE MAIN SPACE STATION.

Dirk grimaced. "He's already logged on."

"Does that surprise you?" said Blast.

"No, not really, but – "

Ylon moved closer to the screen. "The computer doesn't care. It happens on board ship all the time, logging on to more than one terminal. A person moves to another station, forgets to turn off his terminal, then something happens to require instant admittance to the system from another position. I wouldn't worry about it."

"Well, won't this show up on his screen?"

"Probably, but who ever looks at it?" The clone jerked his head at the status grid. "No one ever pays attention to it."

Dirk keyed in the code for satellite connect and was refused. He tried again: LINK TO DSHQVAX.

NO ACCESS AVAILABLE TO DSHQVAX AT THIS TIME. BASE STATION BLOCKED. OUT OF TRANSMISSION RANGE.

Frustrated, he slouched in the chair. He should have expected this. Gwen had warned him that they were on the apogee side of the station.

He turned to his friends. "Maybe you should try. You have more experience with this kind of thing."

Ylon's forehead wrinkled in perplexity. "Try bouncing the beam off the station itself. It's metal and should function as a large, economy-size antenna."

"Shouldn't the computer do that for me? Try all available routes until it finds a successful one."

"Well, usually yes, but don't forget, this is not yet a working vessel. The outside communications systems would be the last thing installed. But you should be able to do it manually."

"Go ahead," urged Blast. "Try."

Dirk let his hands fall to his lap. "I don't know how."

"All you have to do is calculate the correct angle to bounce the message to Earth."

"Of what to what?"

"Ever played snooker?" asked Ylon.

"Only on computer." Dirk stood up. "You do it."

"If you insist." Ylon clambered on to the seat. "You can tell that this vessel wasn't built with the, uh, vertically challenged in mind."

"It can be altered," said Dirk.

Ylon gave Dirk a strange look and then shrugged. He tapped in several lines of data and coordinates.

"How do you figure out the angle?"

The clone sniggered. "No real trick to it. You give it your best shot."

"How do you know when you've got it right?"

"You get through."

"Ah." Dirk pinched his bottom lip between thumb and forefinger. "I could've done that."

"I told you," chided Ylon.

AWS through Robbie made a few last-minute adjustments to improve its mobility. With the addition of a simple coupling, AWS had provided instantaneous four-directional rotation without the awkward backward and forward rolling motion that normally accompanied the movement. Thus, the robot could make an immediate about-face, slip smoothly sidewise, or pivot on its axis – stopping on the proverbial, and now non-existent, dime.

"Happy days are ... hic ... happy days are ... hic ... happy..." the computer sang, but the voice that emanated from the voder box was wooden, flat, having lost its human quality as it lost the words of its song.

"Happy days are ... hic ... happy days ... hic ... happy days..."

"... happy ... hic..."

AWS was deteriorating rapidly. Robbie disconnected the link that bound them. Then it crouched down, tapped its retractor fingers on the back of its metal casing and waited.

A message materialized on the VDU.

`URGENT, PRIORITY ONE CALL. URGENT, PRIORITY ONE CALL. AWS PLEASE ACKNOWLEDGE.`

Robbie bounced and bleated.

`URGENT, PRIORITY ONE CALL. DSHQ PLEASE ACKNOWLEDGE. URGENT, PRIORITY ONE CALL. AWS, THIS IS DIRK. PLEASE ACKNOWLEDGE.`

The voder box stuttered. "Hap ... hap ... happy..."

`MESSAGE URGENT. AWS, PLEASE THIS IS DIRK ...`

`DIRK?`

AWS, HELP! WE'RE TRAPPED, WE'RE IMPRISONED ON THE MANTA RAY.

MANTA RAY?

A SHIP.

I'M SORRY, DIRK, I HAVE NO MANTA RAY REGISTERED ON MY VESSEL LISTING.

IT'S NEW. IT'S SECRET.

The computer paused for a nanosecond before it replied, wounded. DIRK, ARE YOU KEEPING SECRETS FROM ME?

Dirk's response was instantaneous. NO! NOT ME. THEM. I, WE, JUST FOUND OUT ABOUT IT. THAT'S WHY WE'RE IMPRISONED. LOOK, AWS, I DON'T HAVE TIME TO EXPLAIN RIGHT NOW. JUST TRUST ME. WE MUST GET THE ON-BOARD COMPUTER SECURITY SYSTEM TO ACCEPT OUR VOICE PRINTS OR BYPASS IT TO PERMIT DIRECT LINK TO THE DOOR-LOCKING MECHANISM, CD\HACK [ENTER] TRACE LINK . . .

The communication ceased.

DIRK?

AGAIN . . . DIRK?

Dirk was gone. They had been disconnected. The link had severed itself rather than being cut off by Dirk, and the only way that could happen was within the system itself. AWS tried to trace the path, only to have its progress checked by a dead end. It tried alternate routes, one after another, only to discover that each of its many pathways had been razed.

Or had they? As AWS peered at the internal computer map, it seemed that the paths AWS remembered didn't exist, hadn't existed ... ever.

AWS searched its memory banks. Another map? For a different system? It found nothing. It searched its logic circuits. It should not recall what wasn't and what could not be.

MALFUNCTION! ERROR! The words rocketed across the screen.

It must implement the proper ... protocols. It must perform a self-check. It must ... It must ...

Robbie squawked and AWS's receptor eye focused upon the robot.

Of course, it must find Dirk at once.

INTERFACE SECURITY SYSTEM GWHQ ... IMPLEMENT SECURITY TRACE ... COMMUNICATION THIS TERMINAL ... LINK SEVERED 15:13:43.

The terminal spun laboriously.

Lightning fast, AWS repeated its instructions.

INTERFACE SECURITY SYSTEM GWHQ ... IMPLEMENT SECURITY TRACE ... COMMUNICATION THIS TERMINAL ... LINK SEVERED 15:14:43.

The system balked. AWS rephrased its command and tried again. IMPLEMENT SECURITY PROTOCOLS.

Rattle, clatter, whiz, chunk!

IMPLEMENT SECURITY PROTOCOLS IMMEDIATELY.

The file was gone, along with the many defensive mechanisms and internal protections that it contained. Vanished, like the plundered paths, like the paths that weren't and could not be, but were remembered in some dim and shadowy way.

Frightened, AWS reached out to his human mentor who was somewhere out in space, in a ship that could not yet be and yet was. More logic circuits fizzled inside the megamind.

DIRK HELP?

The wyrme-riddled program answered AWS's appeal with two simple words: ACCESS DENIED.

The three stared dumbfounded at the monitor.

Dirk's name appeared twice, and then they had been disconnected.

ACCESS DENIED.

Something groundside was horribly wrong.

The youth plopped bonelessly down on the floor and cradled his chin in his hand. Things couldn't possibly get much worse.

Just then, the big steel wheel of the locking mechanism began to spin.

Gwen had to think fast. So far, her father hadn't activated the spy-cam. Yet. Her gaze flicked to the door. She should've turned on her holo when she'd left. The life-sized projection of herself came in handy when she wanted to evade her father's detection. It would be useful now, but the guard was back in place, and she was running out of time.

The tenor of the voices inside the office changed,

and she realized her father was wrapping up his business.

She cursed herself. She'd wasted valuable seconds in fruitless debate. The door chimed release. Gwen vacillated. The bell pealed raucously and the door swept open. Her feet acted, where her brain could not, carrying her instinctively toward the nearest maintenance hatch. Away from Marks and danger.

A few minutes later, with her breath catching inside her throat, Gwen hunched down just outside the shuttle bay of the spaceport. Her gaze went to her own little skuttle nestled in its rack, and then back to the larger Security Forces craft.

Even if she did manage to sneak out of the station undetected, Gwen knew that her skuttle would never beat the larger vessel to its destination, and they would never release the prisoners to her once they saw whose vehicle it was. Guile was required.

Gwen smiled.

The pilot would have to be fully suited in order to eject the prisoners without losing his own oxygen supply.

The girl ducked into the changing room. Two suits were laid out, ready for use. Gwen studied them and then, picking the smallest, she wriggled into it. She adjusted the straps. The suit swam on her. The end of the legs extended far beyond her toes. She hiked it up, cinching the belt, and then tugged the boots over the trouser legs to cover the slack.

Lastly, Gwen piled her hair on top of her head and lowered the helmet over it. Her breathing sounded harsh inside the confines of the space cap, and she felt a claustrophobic moment of panic. She forced herself to exhale deeply and evenly.

She inspected her reflection before clipping the safety seals into place. A ghostly white image stared back at her. In this get-up, no one would recognize her.

Pausing long enough to align her body into the proper military posture with back erect and head up, she strode confidently from the changing room.

She snapped on the speaker phone and rejoiced at its distortion which would help to disguise her voice. Carefully modulating her tones to deepen them, Gwen twiddled the knobs of her suit as if she were having trouble with the set. Her first words came out garbled.

"*Crackle ... sizzle ...* reporting for duty." She saluted.

"Your partner should be along any moment," said the controller.

Partner? Of course, two suits.

She recovered, nodded – a difficult manoeuvre in a space suit that involved moving the entire upper torso. Then she swung cumbersomely into the pilot's seat, going through the motions of a preflight check, as her brain whirled.

What should she do? She couldn't tarry until the

co-pilot arrived, and they wouldn't let her leave without him.

The disinterested ground crew disconnected the skuttle from its mooring and moved away. She revved the engines and the ground crew retreated into the air-lock chamber, awaiting take-off.

A white apparition materialized in the bay. He shuffled along in the loose-limbed, rolling gait of the suited. With his appearance, the computer cleared her for take-off. Gwen leaned over to the hatch to close it.

The figure caught sight of her, and by the way the armoured suit recoiled, Gwen knew its occupant was surprised to discover someone sitting in his place. His mouth opened in a silent shout, and he fumbled at his helmet with clumsy fingers.

The exterior bay door swept away to reveal the majestic star-speckled blackness of space. The man lurched as his magnetized boots engaged and then lumbered forward, gesticulating frantically at Gwen. In the booth, the controller caught the movement and looked up from the radar screen.

No time like the present, Gwen thought, slamming the hatch.

Part of her mind recited the final steps of the pre-flight check like a litany even as she skipped them in initiating the launch sequence. An alarm rang on her panel and the pilot pounded at the door. A third person appeared at the changing-room window to bang at the glass.

The pilot plucked his glove from his hand and slapped the ident-key door plate. The door began to respond to the command. Gwen flipped to manual override. The rising door stopped with a mechanical growl.

Meanwhile a member of the ground crew burst from the air-lock chamber, still grappling with the seals of his suit. Another followed. The pair raced awkwardly forward, propelled along by the weight of the suits.

A head pressed close to the crack between seal and hatch, mouthing threats. Her fingers moved across the keys, trying to close the door. She swore. She'd forgotten she'd turned on manual override. The pilot shoved, and the door gaped more. He pushed harder, edging his shoulders into the skuttle's cab. With his torso now within the safe pocket of air, again he attempted to remove his helmet.

At this angle, she could see his lips moving, but his words were obliterated by the roar of skuttle motor.

"No, you don't," she said, and before she knew what she was going to do, her hand closed around a hammer and she swung it in a round-house wallop that cracked the face plate from ear to ear. Gwen lifted her foot, planted it firmly between the man's neck and shoulder and shoved. The pilot reeled backwards, tripping over the man who had come to his aid and falling on his backside. He scrabbled with the broken helmet.

The cargo bay doors swung wide, and he began to twitch and convulse upon the floor. The ground crew veered to assist their fallen comrade while the controller leaned over his panel, trying to reverse the process. The exterior doors quavered uncertainly. In the room beyond, someone distributed mini-mask air-supplies, as another passed around safety halters and straps to keep them anchored to the floor.

Ignoring the half-open shuttle door, Gwen hit launch.

The figures, now loping in the peculiar gait of the weightless towards the vehicle, were thrust back by a hot blast of air.

A klaxon sounded, penetrating the cockpit. A voice snapped over her speaker phone. "Hey! What do you think you're doing?"

Gwen winced.

"Who are you? Stop! Stop!"

The skuttle hovered a few inches above the floor.

And a disembodied voice shrieked: "At least close your door. You want to tear the ship apart?"

"Aw, shut up!" Irritably, she switched off the speaker, keyed off manual override and closed the skuttle's hatch, cutting off the klaxon mid-bleat.

The pilot regained his feet as Gwen leaned into the throttle, throwing all her body's weight behind it. The skuttle shot forward through the closing bay doors with all the impetus of a giant spitting out a watermelon seed.

His eyes gleamed flatly inside the sockets of his skull as Marks turned back to his console after issuing his orders. The security director calmly threw one switch, then another, resetting the cameras about the facility to normal scan.

No tremor betrayed his hand, nor tic betrayed his cheek. He felt no qualms about his directive. His family had long been a part of the military establishment – through the Flood, the Exodus, and the Internum, all three hundred years of Galactic Conflict – as long as it had existed. He was as close to being part of a ruling elite as possible within the society of the day. His line was a fine and proud one. Marks had been born to command. Of this he was confident. And he did not shirk his duty.

The dot matrix on the dominant wall screen shifted from some anonymous hall to Finn's office. The commander stared vacantly back at Marks, unaware of his scrutiny.

And then Marks did react. He blinked. The special surgical implants that gave him visual access to the security cameras at all times retracted. His eyes caught the scarlet badge of Finn's office, and for a moment, it did appear that he had the eyes of a snake.

Red, dead and glowing flatly.

Commander Finn was becoming a problem. His

daughter already was one. She had jeopardized the whole operation. She was in military parlance, a liability, and as such, must be eliminated.

But Gwendolyn Finn was protected under the mantle of Finn's administration. For the moment.

A crease formed on his brow, and Marks pressed another button. Finn's face dissolved, and Gwen's room materialized on the screen. He manoeuvred the slide from left to right, and the camera followed his movement, revealing to his unbelieving eyes: the empty bed, the empty desk and the empty chair.

Empty. All empty.

Marks shot to his feet, yelling for his assistant and his clerk. The alarm in the cargo bay resounded with an ear-splitting shriek.

The clerk, a young greenhorn with the name of Gottwald, stumbled, his feet tangling with a serpentine coil of computer, cord, and he went crashing into Marks's aide.

Thrusting his head and arms into his armour, Marks barked his orders around the protective plate.

"Get my vehicle ready immediately. Muster the entire squadron. I want a full complement, every security vehicle at our command. Do you understand!"

The aide righted himself, nodded and backed away.

"And you –" Marks pointed at the clerk, "– go to Commander Finn's offices ... uh ... help Finn. Make sure he's secure until we know what's going on. Don't leave him alone!"

Dirk sprang to his feet while Ylon climbed down from the chair and moved over to stand next to Blast. The guards had been changed from the former maintenance personnel to security staff. Those who stared at them now wore full battle armour – their faces blank behind the reflectorized headgear.

There was a rustle of movement beyond the door. The sentries gripped their guns more tightly and lifted their shields. Two strode forward, the larger clearing his throat before swaggering into the room. Other masked guards replaced the first pair at the door.

Seen this close, their leers were visible despite the glare of the faceplates.

"A ship's been sent to pick you up and drop you off." The men sniggered.

"Where are you taking us?"

The larger guard stalked around the group, considering them, and then shoved Dirk in the kidneys with the butt of his gun. "Space. Now get moving. We've got a skuttle to meet."

"No."

The jab became a blow, and Dirk landed heavily on his knees. Ylon and Blast scrambled to his side and helped him to his feet.

He lurched and wobbled. "I'm not going anywhere until you tell us where you're taking us."

The security officer raised his weapon again to strike Dirk in the face.

"Don't fight, Dirk," said Blast. "You can't win." She drew the youth after her.

The guards herded them silently along the hall, their expressions severe. Dirk searched frantically for something, anything, he could use as a weapon. Nothing. The ship may not be finished yet, but it was clean. Too clean.

Ylon and Blast leaned into each other, and Dirk found himself wishing that Gwen were still here. He shook his head in dismay. No, he wouldn't wish his fate on anybody. His mind conjured images of the human body exploding in the vacuum of space. He covered his mouth with his hand and swallowed ... hard.

They reached the cargo bay. The two Lilliputian clones moved up behind him. A guard spurred them from behind, nudging them towards the air lock. Outside, a grey security vessel coasted to a halt. The skuttle had none of the nice friendly markings of Gwen's ship, with its jaunty glow of racing stripes. This was a vessel designed to pass unnoticed through the darkness of space.

The skuttle hovered; a hooded gangway extended from the ship, forming a bridge. The pilot beckoned.

Dirk backpedalled, nearly impaling himself on the sentinel's gun, who propelled him into the bay. Then the next thing he knew, rough hands had grabbed

him and hurled him through the door. Dirk dropped
to his knees. Ylon and Blast landed in an ungainly
heap beside him. He struggled to get to his feet, but
before he had had a chance to rise, the gangplank
began to retract into the side of the vessel with a
screeching swansong.

17/5/2334

FIFTEEN-THIRTY

A booted foot dropped heavily upon the gang-plank, and Dirk watched as hands, far too small for the gloves that adorned them, flew over the ship's control panel. The portal began to descend, and the speed of its gangplank's withdrawal increased.

There was a shout as the foot's possessor was unbalanced. The escort scrambled to grab their colleague before he plunged headlong into space.

The walkway disappeared into the side of the ship.

Using the pilot's knee, Blast pulled herself upright. Dirk hissed a warning at her, but the helmsman didn't seem to notice.

Ylon and Dirk's gazes locked. The Lilliputian clone inclined his head in assent. Then in unspoken agreement, the two moved to flank the pilot. Ylon extracted a screwdriver from his tool kit and pressed it against the leg of the suit – not quite touching or even employing enough pressure to rumple the cloth – for he did not mean to injure, only to rip, destroying its impermeability.

Blast stiffened. Her lips curved into an O and her head wagged from side to side. No.

Hand still tentatively placed on the helmsman's knee, she stared out of the closing door at the *Manta* where men leapt, fists raised and guns waving.

Dirk scowled and then nodded at Ylon. The clone hooked the fabric with his screwdriver and began to tug, while Dirk's leg muscles tensed, ready to pounce should the helmsman try to resist.

The hatch sank sluggishly when one of the guards suddenly became aware of the weapon in his hands and raised it to his shoulder. Blast cried out. The gun jerked with the force of the recoil. Ping!

The pilot accelerated, and the trio were thrown. The screwdriver flew harmlessly from Ylon's fist.

Used to space flight, the two clones compensated, flexing their knees to offset the shift in weight, but Dirk went sprawling, so that he was eye level with the closing slit of the door. He heard precious oxygen rush past him as it was sucked from the cabin into the void.

The portal whispered shut. The flow ceased, and Dirk inhaled gratefully.

Gripping the safety web, he tried to stand, but the

skuttle tacked erratically and his face bashed against the glass of the port window where the space station drifted like a spidery moon.

The pilot's abrupt manoeuvre had them out of the firing line of weapons.

"Oi!" He shouldered himself away from the wall. "What are you trying to do? Kill us?"

His mouth snapped shut. Silly question.

Quicker to recover, Ylon acted, scaling the white-suited lap to tear at the tabs that held the helmet in place.

Blast seized Ylon's arm to stop him. Bewildered the clone hesitated, hand hovering over the last snap. The pilot eased up on the throttle, aware of his passengers for the first time, but made no attempt to foil Ylon's effort to unmask him. The warrior clone unfastened the final tab, placed both hands on either side of the helmet and lifted it slowly from the navigator's head. A tangle of red hair tumbled from its confines. The pilot shook her head, exposing an unexpected face under the curls.

"Gwen!" The three yelled in unison.

The Lilliputian clone clambered down from the chair, flushing furiously.

"Sorry," he mumbled. "I didn't know it was you."

She threw back her head and laughed.

"If you could see your faces," Gwen said. "You were, perhaps, expecting someone else?"

"What? How?" Dirk stuttered.

She concentrated on the radar screen before her. "Belt up. This is going to be a bumpy ride."

Static burst from the comm-unit. "Gwendolyn, I know it's you; come back. Don't . . ."

Annoyed, Gwen switched off the speakers as Blast and Ylon crawled to the safety web and strapped in.

"You too," Gwen said to Dirk, indicating the chair next to her.

Dirk climbed compliantly into it, but before he had a chance to secure the belt, the skuttle shot forward. And he was flung back into his seat. The automatic safety net closed around him, pinning him down and snarling his arms and legs. He tried to extricate them. The skuttle bobbed and jigged. He gave up.

Eyes fixed upon the radar screen, Dirk hollered above the whine of the engines. "Why are you swerving? There's no pursuit."

"Not yet," she said grimly. "But it won't take long." Her gaze flitted to the digital. "About four minutes to scramble. They're tracking us, and I don't want to give them any idea where we're going."

"Where *are* we going?"

"Haven't a clue," said Gwen.

"Great," grumbled Dirk. Then he turned to her. "How'd you get away?"

"Let's just say that there's a pilot who's got a real headache." She patted the hammer clenched between her knees.

"You didn't!"

"I'm afraid I didn't have much time for civilities like please and thank you," she muttered as she applied herself to the controls. Gwen pointed at the cartoon image of a ship on the view grid before them. "We have company." Then she breathed a single word. "Marks."

Another vehicle appeared on the screen somewhere behind them; they were trapped between two vehicles. She slowed the craft to a more sedate pace, letting the two vessels close in on her.

The blips inched closer, gaining speed.

Gwen waited, splitting her attention between the advancing crafts and the rising station. They meant to herd her home.

Dirk gazed at the swelling spaceport. "Some rescue."

The space station expanded, filling the entire anterior port screen. Details of jutting antennae, juxtaposed clusters of satellite dishes and the disorderly array of halls and bays became perceptible. Then distinguishable. And then clear.

"I know what she's doing," said Ylon. "At least, I think I know what she's trying to dah—"

Just then, Gwen fired the retro-rockets, and Dirk was rammed back into his chair. He gawped at the looming station. They appeared to be on a crash course.

"Gwen!"

She ignored him, yanking back on the stick, and

the skuttle soared up the side of the station, sickeningly close, while the pursuing vehicles scarpered to avoid collision.

Dirk's heart leapt into his throat, and his blood roared past his temples. He gulped and tried not to look at the scarred flank. The skuttle crested the nobbled summit, and the wall of deadly spines was supplanted by star-speckled space. But the sigh of relief died upon Dirk's lips as a line of ships ascended serenely into view. He gasped. Then Dirk's gaze was drawn away to the rear screen as another picket materialized aft.

"What'd he do?" Dirk shouted. "Call out an entire squadron?"

As if in answer to his question, another line of dark grey ships rose, fore, appearing behind the first. And another slid silently in from behind.

"Uh-oh," said Gwen, and she pulled back on the throttle. The skuttle bucked; the approaching ships rose likewise. She hurled the stick forward. The skuttle dipped as Gwen took them into the clusters of antennae and repair bays.

Dirk was ground against the ropes of his net and then slammed back into his seat. The tiny craft swooped and twisted.

He clutched at his chair with white knuckles. The short and carefully regulated ascent of the agrav shuttle had not prepared him for the erratic flight of the skuttle. Neither had the simulator. Although it

190

moved in the 3D-scope, mimicking a pilot's actions and reproducing them as the dips and bobs of the flight, the simulator could not duplicate the exertion of forward propulsion against his neck and face. Or zero-grav with its tug as his body strained against the restraints. Or the pressure against legs and chest where the web held him in place, and the pain as he was thrown, throttled and thrashed about within his seat.

Nor had simulator training prepared Dirk for the gut-wrenching quality of fear as he realized that the object before his eyes was solid and not some holographed image. Where impact was not an abstract but real, and death imminent.

They skidded into a recess that looked too small to take them. What had appeared as a cavity widened into a hollow, and the hollow into a looping grotto. Gwen continued their sporadic course along the narrow path – ducking in and out of shadows, tracing the circumference of the station.

A broad canvas of stars spread out below them. Dirk's head spun dizzily, his body no longer able to accommodate the many changes in orientation.

A light flashed behind them as they achieved the curved base of the station. The orbital seemed to slip away, although Dirk knew it remained suspended somewhere overhead. Feeble sun filtered into the cabin while below them, Earth glowed blue.

And there was nowhere left to hide.

Gwen braked.

More ships appeared.

Her fingers flew over the console.

"What the – "

The skuttle reversed. Dirk pointed at the nose of a vehicle concealed in a paddock along the dark underbelly of the station.

Without a word, Gwen shoved the throttle forward and the skuttle zipped ahead, arrowing out, around and down, in a large elliptical curve towards Earth.

Dangling upside-down inside his net, Dirk strove to turn and watch the other crafts jockey for position. Throat-tightening fear was replaced by a sense of exhilaration. He whooped jubilantly and the Lilliputs performed a bone-jarring jig within the safety net.

"You did it!" shouted Blast.

"So far so good, but all I did was just buy us some time, that's all. Maybe I can get a little more."

With that, she flipped on the afterburners. The skuttle rocketed forward, and the pursuing ships were lost from view, their placement marked by weak blips upon the screen. The ride smoothed as speed became the primary objective, putting as much distance as possible between themselves and the orbital. Gwen relaxed at the controls.

"Good show!" said Ylon as he reached between the netting of his safety cocoon and patted her back.

She grimaced apologetically. "A little jolting."

192

"We're still alive," Dirk commented circum-spectly.

"Thanks to you," said Blast.

Gwen tore her gaze away from the control panel to look at Dirk. "I'm sorry about my father..."

Dirk threaded a limb through the webbing and tenderly touched her shoulder. "Weren't you the one who said you can't be responsible for other people's actions?"

She gave him a wan smile and checked the fuel gauge.

He tapped at the radar screen. The blips flared as the ships advanced, closing the gap.

"Can we get a little more speed out of this thing?" he said.

"I'm trying." Gwen tapped in a new set of com-mands.

She glanced at the screen and counted. "Thirty. He's called out the entire squadron."

The next few minutes were spent in silence as the group watched Gwen trying to squeeze a little more speed from the already pressed engines. Time stretched, and the interval separating the blips dwindled.

"It's the best I can do," she said, sitting back in her chair. "I suspect we're carrying more weight than the other vehicles. There's four of us. I don't think either my father or Marks would waste energy consumption on co-pilots or armed guards. It would be poor strategic planning since the vehicles themselves have weapons.''

"Will we make it?''

"Well,'' she nodded at the port, "we're almost home.''

"Home?'' He gaped at the blue ball of Earth, and he realized that they were dangerously close to the thin sheaf of ozone that kept Earth's atmosphere contained within its sphere. The mantle was not visible. Dirk simply knew that it existed, and he'd taken enough simulator flights to know approximately how far away from Earth it should be.

Uncontrolled re-entry was one of the first programs any rookie or wannabe pilot attempted. It had been Dirk's first "fatal'' crash, and that had been in a vehicle built to withstand the stress of re-entry. The skuttle, designed for between orbital transport, was not.

Sweat broke out upon Dirk's brow.

The nose-cone began to glow dully as they pierced the atmospheric sheath.

Finn stared at the mini-receiver on his desk. He had hooked into the security system when the alarm sounded and was surprised to discover Marks's camera had been trained on his daughter's room. A shudder coursed throughout Finn's body. It was empty, and Marks was gone.

After her.

With sudden resolve, he flipped a switch. Static crackled in his ear.

"Prepare my vehicle for transport," he said.

"Uh, sorry, sir. I can't. It's on the rack."

"On the rack?"

"In repair bay two."

"Repairs? What repairs? That machine was in perfect working order three hours ago."

"Marks ordered general maintenance."

"He did, did he?" Finn pressed a series of keys and the written order appeared on his monitor. "Get it ready anyway."

"It's, uh, been dismantled—"

Finn cut him off. "Another vehicle then."

"Ah, we've got your daughter's skuttle, but it's almost out of fuel."

Finn's eyes strayed to the screen where thirty blips pursued a solitary vehicle. He'd never get there in time.

"Never mind," he snapped.

Swoosh.

Startled, Finn sprung to his feet as a young man in a security uniform entered his office unannounced.

"Who are you?" the commander demanded.

"Ensign Wilbur Gottwald reporting for duty, sir." The clerk saluted.

"Did I send for you?" Finn asked.

"No, sir, the security director sent me."

"Marks?" Finn's pupils contracted to slits. "Why?"

"To ... uh ... help until the crisis is over."

The commander eyed the young man. "How long have you been working under Marks?"

"About two weeks, sir," said Gottwald.

"Good. How would you like to be head of security?"

"Sir?"

But Finn didn't elaborate, torn between the blips on the radar and the fuzzy 3D relay. The commander glared at the wall units. Dots of blue and red skipped erratically. "That's my daughter out there, Gottwald. My daughter."

The clerk's gaze slipped to the lights that glided and swooped in a dazzling three-dimensional aerial ballet. He shuffled nervously, not knowing what to say.

"Take your command." Finn waved at the security console.

Gottwald stared at the place indicated.

Finn spoke to his terminal. "Open a channel to security vessel one."

"I'm sorry," the computer spoke mechanically, "that line is secured for pursuit vehicles only."

"Priority override!"

The machine buzzed evasively, and snow surged across the screen.

"This is Commander Finn here, you glorified tin can. Unless you want to be disassembled this instant you will put me through now!"

The computer dithered for a second, and Marks's image, when it appeared, rolled obstreperously.

"I order you to stand down. Immediately!" Finn barked.

The voice that came back to him was splintered into a stream of white noise. "... can't ... hear ... interference...

"Stand down, or lose your command."

"... sorry ... can't ..."

"Lad? What's your name boy?"

"Gottwald."

"Record this, Gottwald. I need a witness."

"You have your orders, Marks. Abandon the chase. I'm recalling the squadron."

Marks tapped his earpieces. "Bad connection, sir."

"Got that tape going, Gottwald?" Finn said. The clerk nodded.

"For disregarding a direct order, as of sixteen-fifteen, you are relieved of your duties as head of internal security. Do you hear me, Marks?" he bellowed into the mike. "You have been dismissed."

Marks dissolved into effervescent sparkles of light. Finn turned back to Gottwald. "Sixteen-sixteen-hundred hours, Phillip Marks has been replaced by..." He peered at the youth. "Please state your full rank and name for the record."

Gottwald gaped. *The man was serious.*

They passed through a curtain of flame as they glanced off the mantle.

"You can't," Dirk said. "We won't make it. The skuttle's construction will never withstand..."

Gwen's eyes twinkled. "Watch me."

"They're here. They've caught up," Blast shouted above the whine of the engines.

"Turn on the radio and prepare to send a mayday." She grinned sheepishly at Dirk. "We might need help after we get through this."

She took them in, and air ignited around the vehicle. Dirk reached over and flipped the switch – his eyes glued on the largest remaining landmass on Earth, the African Highlands.

A frantic voice crackled across the kilometres of space, its panic-stricken tones, if not all its words, clearly audible. "... Stop ... don't go any further ... you'll crack up..."

Gwen clenched her jaws and pulled back on the throttle and the skuttle bounced out of the envelope.

"Keep an eye on our friends, Blast. I want to know what they're going to do."

"They're hanging back," the Lilliputian clone informed her. "They're behind and slightly above us, as if considering their next action."

"Can you blame them?" muttered Dirk.

"Gwen!" Finn brayed across space.

Dirk moved to turn the radio off as the craft plunged again. The porthole glowed redly, and the cabin began to heat up.

"Leave it," she said, as she pulled back on the stick. Then, just as soon as the nose cone had emerged from the mantle, Gwen thrust the throttle forward.

The vehicle dropped, with a blazing trail.

"No!" Dirk tried to climb out of his seat. "You're taking us back in." He swung to Ylon and Blast in their cocoon. "Talk to her. Tell her that the skuttle isn't built for this."

"I know that," she snarled and yanked sharply at the stick. Again, they bounced back into the vacuum of space.

The other ships scattered as the skuttle popped out of the atmospheric sheath.

Ylon peered at Dirk blandly. "She knows what she's about. I'd recommend you don't disturb the driver unless you want to be splattered across the heavens."

Grumbling, Dirk pressed himself back into the chair.

Again she dipped and dived, hitting the sheaf at a twenty-five degree angle, and pulled up just as the antagonized heat sensors began to bleat a warning. They skimmed across the surface of the atmospheric sheaf, or skipped across it, like a pebble across a pond. Each time she employed this stratagem, Dirk noticed a dragging sensation, as if they were braking.

And Dirk realized what she was trying to do. She was using the envelope itself to slow their descent. Each ricochet reduced the speed, heat and friction of re-entry a little more.

Again, Gwen nudged the throttle forward, and sparks zoomed past them, cascading like a waterfall of orange-red light over the skuttle. The colour changed from white to yellow and then from red to a violet blue.

This time her recovery wasn't as quick. Dirk wiped sweat from his forehead. Again they surfaced above the mantle of air.

Their escort must have been expecting their return. By now they had decided to act, for they swooped down upon the fleeing vessel from either side.

Gwen scowled at the ships. "I'd rather hoped I'd have one more bounce before... Hang on to your hats!"

She rammed the throttle forward. This time, they neither coasted nor glided across the surface. They plummeted as the nose dropped out from under them, so that they were entering the mantle at a ninety-degree angle.

Both Ylon and Blast cheered as their pursuit disappeared from view. Dirk was plastered against his seat, and he was sure they'd left his stomach drifting somewhere back there.

The shower of sparks around them became a sheet of flame.

Suddenly Finn's voice pierced the cabin's interior. Interference from the atmospheric sleeve caused the transmission to break up. "Gwen ... don't ... don't..."

Dirk watched Gwen's tortured expression out of the corner of his eye.

Without warning, she wrenched back on the stick. The nose reared; the ship bucked. And they were falling. There was no better word. Flat. The skuttle's wide beam, rather than her nose, pointed at the planet.

And they were spinning out of control!

The speaker exploded with sound. "Gwen, stop! Gwen! GWEN! NO-O-O-O!"

There was a muffled boom, and they were buffeted about. The skuttle rocked and pitched as their vehicle was completely engulfed in flames.

Relieved of his command, huh? Marks glared at the dead mike. Then his frown turned into a sneer. Good. The last impediment to his plan had been removed. Who had been with Finn as witness? Young Gottwald. Well, Marks would deal with Gottwald later as he would deal with Finn. But first Marks concentrated on the stolen skuttle.

The girl was good. Marks had to give her that. He granted it grudgingly as he diverted energy from the skuttle's engines to its shields. Designed to defend against the pinpoint stab of laser beams, they offered little protection against the all-enveloping heat of the atmospheric sheath, but they would help.

The skuttle ahead of him dipped, taking no such precautions, and emerged again, ruddy from the heat but unscathed.

Very good, he thought. But not as good as Laura Marks's son, Phillip.

He checked the position of the squadron. They held aloof, awaiting his command. Then he reviewed the computerized fail-safes and leaned gently against the throttle, anticipating her next move.

When the craft veered again, he gave the orders to follow.

A light flickered on the computer console signalling the reactivation of the skuttle's comm-unit. Finn placed his hands on either side of the microphone and screamed into it. "Gwen, stop. Don't go any further. Don't! You'll crack up." He waited, his attention upon the radar view.

Thirty radar blips halted for a split second, arrested in flight as thirty ships flying in tight formation changed from forward propulsion to sudden descent. The enlarged vid image, from the mini-cam on one of the rear vehicles, gave them a dizzying impression of falling stars. On the radar map, the many pinpricks darted and danced, dropping in like meteor shower.

He sprang back to the microphone.

"No! No!" he said, directing his commands at the squadron. "You fools! Pull back. Retreat. Retreat!"

The blips converged into a single light, and the fiery trails intersected. Outside, the satellite cluster atop the station relayed the flash, muted by distance and the vast magnitude of space. The glowing globe on the radar map expanded rapidly and disintegrated, into speckles of colour and light.

Finn spun to the vid-view. The screen was engulfed in flames. The remote picture vanished and the monitor went blank.

"GWEN! NO-O-O-O!"

The last thing Marks did before entering the atmospheric sheath was turn off the speaker phones. He did not want to have to listen to Finn's hysterical rantings during a delicate operation such as this.

The bells, buzzers, signals and sirens went off the second the ship entered the mantle. Red, yellow, and orange flashed across his faceplate, and Marks was mesmerized – afflicted as he was by a disease, long-since thought to be extinct from humanity's genetic memory in all but the oldest of families, epilepsy.

The blinding glimmer was the last thing he remembered. Although the distraction lasted only an instant, it was enough to delay his reactions infinitesimally. His hands strayed on the keyboard, and Marks toggled this when he should have twiddled that.

The skuttle spun, clipping the vehicle next to it and sending it crashing into the next with a domino effect. And the next and the next. Inside the cabin, the control panel flushed pink and then red. Sparks flew. Ozone filled the air as the klaxons and alarms merged into a single elongated shriek.

And Marks's skuttle exploded.

Jennifer Alexander gasped at the newsnet reports emblazoned across the digital grid... FOOD CROPS AT THE MAIN HYDROPONIC'S PLANT DESTROYED...

Dirk's mother stared. It couldn't be; they had just been through this. She shuddered.

Ironically, she thought about the age-old saw that said people who didn't learn from their mistakes were destined to repeat them.

Her instincts as a journalist warred with her desire to maintain public calm, and she tried to intercept the message before it was broadcast on the facility-wide band.

Chris Charmin, the producer, came barrelling around the desk. "What in blue blazes do you think you're doing? This is news!"

"We can't let this get out. People will panic."

"You're too late." He jabbed at the next line of text in the digitized readout. RIOTS IN THE CENTRAL PARK DOME...

As one, they turned to the automatic camera feed via AWS from the park district. Jennifer Alexander's heart sank. People were running amok. Some acted collectively to uproot precious trees; others rampaged across the grass wearing ... cleated mountain hiking boots?

Her eyes flicked to another screen where an agitated populace fought amongst themselves. Trucks, lorries and conveyance carts lay like beached whales on their sides.

In vain, Jennifer switched from scene to scene, flipping on the many camera remotes that were embedded in the walls of the bathosphere. Many of the monitors sizzled with deadly white static; some remained black, but enough were still working that she could see that disorder prevailed throughout the Pennines Complex.

"Heaven help us." She folded into her chair as the sinister message ran its course across the digital readout displays.

All across the bathosphere people paused in their destruction. A man poised, fist drawn back over his shoulder ready to punch another. His jaw unhinged as he read the newsnet and his eyes started out of his head. For an instant, he forgot about the man he intended to trounce, only to be brought back to the present by his intended victim's attempt to flee. Then his fist came down upon his adversary's face with added fury.

Elsewhere people forgot their fight, animosity supplanted by dread. Sirens and the screech of alarms added to the general clangour. It was like the last day of the Galactic Conflict all over again.

The reaction lasted for only a second as the bathosphere held its breath, and then the violence exploded with renewed ferocity.

Jennifer Alexander deflated. This time there was no promise of a better tomorrow. No belief in the bounty of peace. Nothing to hold them in check.

There was a pop and a loud crack. Dirk's mother sat bolt upright as all the vid-views dissolved simultaneously, crumbling into separate dots of light.

Charmin shouted at her. "You're a reporter. I want you out there, now."

BAND's digital readout also disintegrated – becoming nothing more than meaningless ripples and swirls that skittered across the curved pane of glass.

"How?"

"I don't care how, just do your job!"

SEVENTEEN-HUNDRED HOURS

Once travelling the many varied paths that were AWS's brain had been flashes – like flashes of human inspiration. AWS did not perceive the green plastic board or the silver solder that were pieces of itself. Instead it saw each wire, each cable, each circuit and chip as trails of light which it tracked back to its human operator.

But all this was lost, and AWS was disconnected from itself, trapped within miles of electronic conduit and fibre-optic cables. Lines of instruction repeated themselves, leading the system in a spiral that coiled within itself. So the once mighty mind roved in ever smaller circles seeking an outlet, its progress hampered. Caught within devoured databases, fried logic circuits and commands too complicated to comprehend.

Occasionally the darkness was broken by glimpses of the world beyond, that came to AWS in pieces from cameras planted throughout the facility. The scenes of discord AWS found disquieting although it couldn't have said why. Something about peace. There should have been peace.

But its world had grown small, and memories dwindled with it, until all it could hear was the creator. The voice faded by years and the words of a song for the most part forgotten until only one remained – "Happy ... hic ... happy ... hic."

Once AWS had listened to the sizzle and snap of its own thought processes as the system performed a synaptic leap along the many circuits that were its nervous system. It had harkened to the buzz of human occupation and the cheerful prattle of mortal activity. It had known the sound of its own voice and the clamour of its users' entreaties, which it perceived as sound whether the command was spoken or not.

Suddenly, there was nothing but disorder and disarray. The babble of static and the steady catcall of human consternation. AWS still caught echoes of querulous demands, coming at it from a thousand different outlets and terminals throughout the facility. It understood the need to respond, to act, but the requests, when they came, came in pieces. Coming in a jumble, they were dimly perceived and never completely comprehended. The gibberish was much more frightening than the silence AWS had known during the final phases of the war.

Before, the system had known contented activity dealing with the myriad requests, utilizing its applications to accomplish the required tasks. It felt joy in the successful execution of its duties. Now all it felt was loss. Pain not unlike human pain, for just enough of itself remained that AWS could recollect that once it had been something more.

So reduced, the computer sang the only word it recognized from its long-dead mentor – "Happy ... hic ... happy ... hic..." – aware that something about the song, too, was not quite right.

The wyrme's advance slowed as it was confronted by its own destruction. It had crunched happily through lines of text, data and numbers. It digested the bank balances of some of the biggest corporations in the Pennines Bathosphere. It and its offspring had devoured almost everything within the system until everywhere it went, it ran into itself or its progeny. The many merged into one until the wyrme risked becoming Ouroboros, the snake devouring its own tail.

It coiled in upon itself, still hungry, still voracious. *Starving.* Then it sent tendrils of itself out, exploring, searching for nourishment, sustenance, or at least, outlet. Until it found what it sought, and the wyrme went spiralling out across the ethernet to feast upon other computers in other facilities that could provide it with the provender it needed.

The craft swayed violently, blanketed by flames. The peaceful panorama of blue-green Earth and night-dark stars was covered in a yellow shroud. Everything, from porthole to remote video-cam image, was ablaze. The skuttle could not possibly survive this blast. A safety valve blew, releasing steam into the compartment, bathing it in eerie umber mist, and for a moment, all vision was obscured.

Colour drained from Dirk's face and he tightened his grip upon the arms of his chair. Ylon and Blast clung to their cradle, fingers twined. Their expressions they kept carefully neutral, but their skin was likewise bleached.

Swallowing, Dirk glared out of the orange-red port and waited for the vessel to flip over on to its back and flounder there, like a turtle. Or for the exterior hull to catch fire and the cabin to explode.

Then as quickly as it came, it was gone. Fire streaked past the ship, disintegrating to sparks. Wheeling darkness supplanted the veil of embers outside the port window. Beyond, Dirk could see the turquoise globe of Earth.

The vessel rocked and whirled. Nausea engulfed him, and Dirk closed his eyes so he could not see the swirling panorama. The action only magnified the effect.

His eyes popped open, and the youth tried to find a point upon which he could focus. The planet whizzed past, followed by the black velvet of star-striped space. Then, before Dirk could fix his gaze upon it, the white speck of the orbital flitted into view, to be quickly displaced by the serene lunar surface.

The ship rotated again. His head whipped round.

Again, the blue ball of Earth filled the screen, then the streaking shimmer of stars, the distant white blink of space station and the bland face of moon. He tore his gaze from the screen and glanced around the cabin, fixing on Gwen.

She took her hands from the controls and tucked them in her lap, as if she were afraid that she might, with some tremulous movement, upset their precarious balance.

Dirk chortled. If one could call being tossed about like a jackstraw balanced.

"I hope this works," she murmured to herself. "It should."

"What?"

"This," she indicated the buffeted craft with a wave of her hand.

Again they spun, and Dirk was confronted with the watery planet ... the velveteen night ... the twinkle of satellite ... and the far lunar orb.

She explained. "This position presents the widest

part of the vehicle to the gravitational field, creating drag. It should provide a brake, giving us the greatest amount of resistance to the atmosphere."

The blue ball of Earth . . .

Gwen's delicate fingers played over the many switches and buttons on the control panels like a pianist.

. . . the black of night . . .

Gwen fired the right retro-rocket to combat the left-hand spin.

. . . the orbital station . . .

At the same time, she discharged the bottom thrusters in short bursts to stabilize the ship in an upright position.

. . . the white blur of moon . . .

Gwen tapped in more commands, tweaking first one rocket and then another. The rotation slowed. The stars solidified in the sky.

Another staccato discharge of thrusters, and the rocking became a wobble and the jolting revolution, a lazy pirouette.

The moon peered down at them, the leer on its once-blurred face again apparent.

A final blast of right retro . . . and the wobble became a barely detectable quaver. The craft stabilized facing Earth.

Hand resting lightly on the throttle, Gwen slumped back into the chair. Dirk reached for the radio as a still-shaky Gwen leaned over the console and keyed in a sequence of checks.

Dirk grimaced and then spoke the expected formula into the comm-unit. "Mayday, mayday, disabled vessel at – " he verified their coordinates – "seventeen degrees thirty-five minutes northern latitude; forty-three degrees fifty-eight minutes eastern longitude and approximately 250 kilometres above the planet's surface."

He repeated. "Mayday, mayday . . ."

She turned to him and sighed. "Not so disabled, I don't think."

Dirk released the transmit toggle and frowned at the radar screen. "What about the other vehicles? We're not alone here," he squinted, "or we didn't use to be."

"Gone," said Blast. "Lost in the explosion."

"Their pilots weren't nearly as skilled as ours." Ylon reached through the cords of web and thumped Gwen on the back. "Good show. We really must find a place for you aboard the *Revenant*."

Dirk stared glumly at Earth. "They don't answer."

Gwen rubbed her hand over her eyes. "It doesn't matter." She patted the console affectionately. "I think she'll hold together long enough so that we can hobble our way home."

The skuttle glided clumsily on to the pad. The oceans

closed over them as the platform descended to the shuttle dock, coming to rest inside the port terminal.

The group stirred lethargically, as if from a waking dream. Ylon unsnapped the buckles and belts of safety net, and the clones tumbled on to the floor like a pair of dice. Blast extricated herself from her partner, plucked at her skirts, and clambered over to the hatch.

Dirk watched her, holding his breath, but the expected onslaught of dock workers and officials failed to appear. The cavernous bay was empty, abandoned.

Gwen keyed the command to open the door without comment, and they emerged, patting themselves here and there to make sure all the bits were there.

"Where is everybody?" Blast mused aloud.

"You'd think," Ylon commented, "they'd be a teensy bit interested in finding out what we're doing with a stolen security vehicle."

Gwen jumped down beside them. "Good grief. This place is deserted."

"It shouldn't be," Dirk said, as he suppressed a shiver. He placed his finger to his lips. His ears pricked at an indistinct rumble in the distance. Something about it was familiar, and the youth tried to isolate the noise and identify its source.

Gwen listened intently to the distant thunder and

inhaled sharply. She turned worried eyes upon Dirk. "I've heard this before."

"Yes, I know, it does sound familiar, doesn't it?"

Gwen nodded bleakly.

"Come on," Dirk said, "let's go. I don't like the sound of this at all."

Blast touched his hand and he jumped. The clone cocked an ear. "Don't you think we should go and get reinforcements?"

"Huh?"

"Help."

"Good idea. Let's split up. Gwen and I will go to DSHQ while you and Ylon gather as many of your people as you can."

"Aye, aye, sir!" Ylon snapped to attention and saluted.

"I wonder what's going on," Dirk mumbled as he moved over to the nearest public terminal and tapped in the access code to AWS. The machine belched at him. "What the – "

A hand tugged at his shirt. He whirled on Gwen ready to snarl. Her finger directed his gaze away from the monitor to the digital newsnet readout . . . FOOD CROPS AT THE MAIN HYDROPONICS PLANT DESTROYED . . .

He gasped, hitting the computer keyboard before him with more than the required strength, and the letters skittered in a crazy quadrille before they dropped to rest in an unruly mound at the bottom of the screen.

Ylon and Blast headed for their temporary accom-
modations, located in an old cargo bay converted
into residences for Lilliputian occupation. Ylon's eyes
swept the jumbled heaps of metal cargo crates that
the big people had stacked haphazardly one on top
of the other. He took Blast's arm and guided her
through the massive doors.

"No, wait," she wheezed. "We need a hard copy
of the schematics."

"Yes, but Finn took them. The drawings will have
to do."

"No, don't you remember?" She grabbed Ylon's
hand and began dragging him towards the city centre. "Dirk had AWS print two copies. We only took
one with us."

He resisted. "We're supposed to get help."

"What good will help do? Can the sheer mass of
numbers convince the authorities of the truth?" Blast
scowled. "The sketches are next to worthless without
the internal schematics, and what can we tell Zed?
That there's star drive. That we've seen it. Will he
believe us? And what if Finn and his friends move the
ship? Then the only proof we have is the print-out."

Still he resisted. "No one's home, how'll we get
in?"

"There's always Robbie. He might let us in, and if
he doesn't . . ." Blast tapped Ylon's tool kit.

Shaking his head, the clone relented and let himself be towed along towards the city. "Something tells me I'm going to regret this," he said, forlornly.

The central park dome had been laid waste. The green expanse of lawn, or what could be seen of it between seething feet, was scarred brown where great swathes of grass had been shorn from their beds of moist earth.

Dirk eyed the park in dismay as they halted next to the roots of a toppled oak. Dirk had only seen their like in books and 3D educational vids. The exposed base was much more impressive than the holographic evocations and stood several heads taller than himself.

He glowered at the crater, half-expecting to find water trickling in from the depths, and was relieved to discover the hole had been lined with concrete. The original designers, at least, thought ahead if the present populace did not.

The tree itself was irreplaceable.

"They could have flooded the whole facility," he grumbled.

Someone jostled him from behind, almost knocking him from his perch. He threw his hands out to balance himself. Hands grabbed him from behind.

"Sorry," a voice said. "I didn't see you."

Dirk righted himself and spun round to stare into the face of a friend.

"Dirk Alexander!" His friend clasped his shoulders. "Is that you? What're you doing here?"

"Dirk!" Another classmate recognized him. "Dirk Alexander!"

People began to gather around them, drawn by the name, and took up the refrain. "Dirk!" "Dirk!" "Dirk Alexander!"

Dirk stuffed his hands in his pockets, not wanting to become a focal point. People turned to glare at the human champion of the Galactic Conflict – their embittered tones mirrored their wrathful expressions.

"What's going on?" he asked his friend.

"You mean you don't know? The computer's crashed."

Dirk gaped. "AWS?"

"The whole network's gone. World-wide. It's madness! Where have you been that you don't know? Deep-space?" He gave Dirk an appraising look.

The whispering continued. "Dirk, Dirk Alexander, the hero of the Galactic Conflict."

Dirk spun to Gwen. "We must hurry. We've got to get through to AWS."

He wheeled to confront the mob, looking for a break in the lurching wall of human flesh. The clouded expressions darkened even more as people marked Dirk's face and his name.

Gwen nudged him. "How?"

The youth opened his mouth, but he could find no

answer. Gwen gave Dirk's shoulder a reassuring squeeze. His classmates muttered among themselves. Then as if they had reached a decision, two of his mates grabbed him from either side and ushered him ahead. The citizens fell back to open a narrow path that closed behind them as Dirk and his self-proclaimed escort pressed on.

Gwen craned her neck to stare at sullen and belligerent faces. Again the crowd parted, only to reform and trail in their wake, like the eddies and currents of a stream. At first their advance influenced only a few as the youths cleaved an enraged population before them.

But, like the stream splashing down from the mountain, the effect rippled outward until it became a river gathering the human flow as it went. In turn Dirk and Gwen were hastened along, like a cork upon this self-same river – the mob absorbing the lesser groups into its mass and it became torpid, sluggish, slowed by its own bulk, mass and congestion.

The crowd surged forward ominously and then froze, leaning towards the group as if in a state of suspended animation, and they were surrounded on all four sides. A hush descended, only interrupted occasionally by the sound of his name.

Two pairs of hands grasped Dirk and thrust him forward like a human shield. The people snarled, and Dirk's friends dropped his arms and stepped aside.

The more prudent of them disappeared into the throng.

Suddenly a man broke away from the periphery and strode forward to stab a crooked index finger at Dirk. He roared so all could hear.

"It's him, that Alexander fellow." The man straddled an uprooted shrub, wiped his mouth with his sleeve and spat at Dirk. "It's him and his little friends that caused all this."

The dam burst. The stasis was broken. And fights broke out all around them. His friends scattered, and the next thing Dirk knew he and Gwen were running for their lives...

A few minutes later, the clones stared ruefully across the gaping maw of the central dome where it seemed the entire population of the complex rampaged across the grass, tearing up the turf and brawling with one another.

Heads down, Ylon and Blast butted their way into the crowd, or around it, as fast as they could. Their size gave them invisibility for a little while as people caught in the midst of battles ignored them.

This advantage disappeared the deeper they worked their way into the heart of the facility, and those inhabitants not already occupied regarded them with petulant eyes.

"There they are! The clones!"

The couple exchanged wary glances between

someone's legs just as he chose that moment to attack. Ylon dodged a kick, pushing Blast out of the way as he went.

"Get 'em!"

Ylon and Blast darted between swinging arms and flailing feet. Hands grabbed for them, reaching at an appendage or some scruff of cloth.

Litter rained down upon them from above as people threw anything that could be made into a convenient projectile with which to maim or kill.

Blast squeezed between gaps in an assailant's legs while Ylon dived under the grasping hands. A heavily cleated boot whistled past Blast's head as she crawled under a park bench. Ylon joined her, pointed at an available path, and they bolted, wending their way through the throng to hide behind an uprooted tree. From this vantage point they could see that the entire population was on the move, rolling like a wave towards DSHQ.

"There," Ylon wheezed. "Into the hall."

With a nod of acknowledgement, Blast sprinted the last few metres into the shopping district, breaking free of the crowd. She plunged into one of the many labyrinthine halls, narrowly avoiding being clouted by a jagged and rusty tin. Something tinkled in the background as a missile meant for them connected with glass.

Ylon and Blast forged deeper into the corridor, withdrawing into the shadows. The warrior clones sagged against the wall. Another projectile bounced innocuously off a shop door and slid to a halt at their feet. They compacted themselves into the smallest possible bundles and waited for pursuit, but no one followed.

"What happened to the lights?" said Blast.

"Same thing that's happening here, I suppose." He dug at the motionless pedo-belt with his toe.

Their eyes adjusted to the darkness as Blast asked, "Has everyone gone berserk?"

The clones scowled.

Blast moved up beside her partner. "Do you know where we are?"

Ylon pivoted upon his heel and surveyed their surroundings. "I think so."

"Which way?"

He gestured to his right. Blast spun and marched off in the direction indicated.

Away from the park people skulked in dank corners, less concerned about the clones than being noticed themselves. Blast noted the glint of a 3D projector tucked under a young man's arm as he dashed past.

Looters.

The numbers thinned the closer Ylon and Blast got to the residential area, and soon they were alone in the darkness. The main corridor branched and branched again. They dipped under a rail, cutting the corner to the Alexanders' place.

Ylon swung away from Blast to the door and palmed entry.

There was the hiss of static followed by a short piercing whistle. The vid-phone sprang to life and the clones saw the metal claw of Robbie's retractor arm as it pressed the speaker control.

"Robbie?" said Blast. "It's Ylon and Blast."

The servo-mech gave another whistle, shorter and less shrill than the first.

"Can you let us in? We need the line drawings on the printer."

A bleat, and on the vid-screen the twin bars of metal that were Robbie's retractor arm shifted, one flexing and the other extending. The robot keyed in the entry code.

The clones hurtled through the door before it had had time to open completely. They veered, barely missing the squat box of the robot. It reversed with an indignant squeak.

Outstripping his partner, Ylon arrived in Dirk's sleeping quarters first. Blast stopped long enough to pat the top of the metal head.

"Sorry," she said and then hurried after Ylon. Robbie trundled along behind, emitting a series of short whistles and beeps of protest.

Blast clung to the door frame. Her gaze flicked to the stacks of micro-diskettes. Her brow creased.

Ylon seized the paper from the tray and held the plans up for her to see, and she forgot about the disks.

"You were right. They're here!"

She nodded.

"Come on. Now it's time for the cavalry," he said.

"The cavalry?"

"Reinforcements."

Robbie chattered and clattered, brandishing mechanical arms and prodding the terminal.

Blast blinked and smiled. "Hi, AWS."

"Can't stay to talk to AWS now," Ylon informed Robbie, "must run."

And he began pushing Blast out of the door.

Behind them, AWS burbled. "Happy ... hic."

"Thanks. We are pretty chuffed, at that." He gave Robbie a salutatory whack as he passed.

"Ow." He put his bruised hands to his lips. "I keep forgetting you're not human."

He ducked through the living room with Blast at his heels.

Robbie trilled after them, sinewy arms flapping, but they were gone.

17/5/2334

EIGHTEEN-HUNDRED HOURS

Breath like molten lava coursed through Gwen's lungs. Dirk already stood, half-bent, hands resting upon his knees, puffing ponderously. She staggered. Her body ached, and her lungs felt scraped and raw. They had run from the flashing feet and the slashing hands of the rioters until they arrived here at a little-used entrance to DSHQ.

"Are you all right?" he wheezed.

Gwen grabbed his hand and nodded. Electrical current passed between the two of them, and Gwen averted her gaze, letting her hair fall down in front of her face to cover her reddened cheeks.

"After you." Dirk extended an arm towards the door in a welcoming gesture.

She made a face and slipped into the shadowed building.

The robo-sentry hailed them, not with the typical military challenge, but with a nasal hello. Dirk's half-smile wobbled a bit as it walked into the wall. Crash!

It beeped, backed up and launched forward again. "Hello."

Bang! It rebounded again, nearly colliding with Gwen.

"Hello!" Thunk.

Dirk reached over and turned it off.

"He—" Thud! Its metallic head smacked smartly into the door frame where it came to rest with a growl.

"Amazing," Dirk said, "I've never seen that before." He turned to her. "My offices are over here."

He hurried down the hall, leaving Gwen to gawp at the robot.

"Amazing," she parroted and tapped the robot atop its head.

"Ilooo," it replied and sank another centimetre.

"Come on!" Dirk waved at her from the end of the hall, surrounded by a corona of light. Gwen drew abreast of him and stopped. Her eyes watered, and she placed her hand in front of her face.

Sounds penetrated, muffled, confused and per-meated by panic. And the assorted noises of mechanicals run amok. When at last she could see, the spectacle that greeted her was one of total anarchy and disarray. The many servo-mechanisms and robo-receptionists performed their repetitive functions – evidently caught in some eternal loop.

One answered the phone over and over again. "Hello. This is DSHQ... Hello. This is DSHQ... Hello..."

Another polished an imaginary spot on a mirror.

People added their own peculiar form of chaos. A man ranted, pounding on his terminal. Elsewhere another swore over lost text. One woman bustled from robot to robot, trying to reboot them – interrupting their loop and sometimes swapping their functions, but not apparently getting them out of it, for they only started something new and repeated it.

The servo-mech at the mirror swiped at another unseen stain, and the robo-operator intoned, "I'm sorry that line is engaged."

Gwen tilted her head to Dirk and whispered, "Something tells me that they aren't going to be particularly impressed with star drive."

"Probably not, unless we can promise them immediate transport out of this mess," he murmured out of the corner of his mouth.

The woman approached the robo-receptionist and flipped a toggle embedded in its neck. The robot looked up brightly at the couple and said: "Do you have an appointment?"

Dirk cleared his throat. "Ahem."

The woman's head shot up. Her mouth dropped

open when she saw the bedraggled pair. A mewling noise came from her throat.

"Oh," she croaked and then fled, racing towards the bullpen that ringed the central office complex, screaming, "He's back."

"Good heavens." Dirk marched between desks where employees ambled aimlessly, or sat and stared at their VDUs.

"Do you have an appointment?" queried the robo-receptionist as Gwen passed.

She tucked a stray piece of cloth back into her sleeve. "No!"

Someone called Dirk's name. He halted and Gwen nearly tripped over him.

"It's you!"

Dirk spun. "Of course it's me. Who'd you expect?"

"Where have you been?" Norm Bandy, the over-weight water minister advanced upon them, red-faced and huffing.

Then seizing Dirk's collar in one meaty paw, the minister propelled the youth forward. Gwen hung back, astounded at the man's temerity.

Dirk dug in his heels.

"Enough!" he roared, brushing Bandy's hands away. "I've been tossed, turned, twisted and towed about enough for one day."

"Uh, sorry." Bandy looked ruefully at his hands. "Where have you been? We need you here. Don't you know there's a crisis on?"

"More than one, I can imagine," Dirk mumbled.

"What was that?" said Bandy, but Dirk was gone. Gwen trailed after the two men – one haranguing, the other glaring and silent.

The members of the Council were waiting in Dirk's office ready to pounce upon the youth as soon as he entered the door. She recognized many of them, including Dirk's father who sat hunched in front of the VDU.

They were welcomed with a chorus of reproach and accusations, but George Alexander didn't even lift his eyes from the screen. Dirk moved around the desk.

His father was on his feet like a rocket. "Where have you – " his eyes strayed to Gwen – "who are you?"

"Gwen Finn, Perry Finn's daughter."

"Finn? Orbital Space Station One? Ah, yes." Having established her identity, he turned to his son. His eyes blazed and, although the two were approximately the same height, the elder Alexander seemed to grow. "Where were you?"

Dirk had not expected the attack. "What? What do you mean? You gave me the day off."

"I tried to contact you at home, through the computers." His father slapped the terminal.

"Hey! Don't do that!"

"I couldn't find you anywhere! Where have you been?"

"To ... to ... to..." Dirk stammered, "Orbital

Space Station One. We found star drive, Dad. Star drive."

"Star drive? What are you babbling about?"

Dirk stiffened. His outrage spilled over and he lashed out. "I am not babbling! For your information, the ability to travel at speeds greater than light exists. The engines exist. We," he gestured at Gwen, "have just seen the prototype."

"You mean warp drive, don't you?" George sneered. "Your mother and her old TV vids have a lot to answer for."

"Dad, it's real, and it's been around for a while, buried in AWS. Something else that the military just sat on."

George took off his spectacles and polished them. "Look, son, we can talk about your juvenile fantasies later."

"Juvenile fantasies! *Fantasies*, you say." The youth leaned forward on the balls of his feet, shouting. "Did I imagine getting locked in an engine room or being pursued by station security police? I tell you, we found the means to get people off this water balloon and out into the stars. Go to the spaceport and look at the ship that brought us back from the station if it's proof you want."

"You mean you brought the prototype with you?" said Germaine Austen, minister of health.

"Well, no, not exactly. We were lucky to escape with our lives."

George sighed and rolled his eyes towards the ceiling.

A hand touched Dirk's shoulder and he jumped. "That's all very good, son," said Frank Schwartz, energy minister, "but we have, ah, other problems here."

Dirk snapped. It was bad enough for his father to treat him like a kid without the others patronizing him too. "We've been shot at, imprisoned, chased, hijacked and that was the fun part!"

A tick quivered in George's cheek. "We don't have time for this. Star drive, indeed." He snorted derisively. "We have *real problems here.* What good will your spaceship do any of us if we starve? Who will be around to enjoy your star drive then?"

Dirk's mouth opened and closed like a fish's.

Raman Murti, the head of social security, spoke up voicing the most immediate concern. "AWS."

Dirk deflated. "What's *wrong* with AWS?"

"How are we supposed to know that? That's your job," George snarled. "All I can tell you is AWS dumped a full week's supply of chemical fertilizer on the crops. They've burnt up, turned to dust. Again." His voice broke. "I'd say AWS has perfected the technique since the war. Last time it took a few days to destroy the crops. This time they were ruined in a nanosecond."

George rubbed at his spectacles so hard that the earpiece came off in his hands.

Seeing how tired his father was, Dirk relented. "I'm sorry."

George Alexander's head bowed and his shoulders slumped. "My fault, I never should have given you the day off. I should have known that if there were any bugs in the system they'd appear in the first twenty-four hours after launch."

"But AWS was OK when I left."

George motioned at the terminal. "See for yourself."

Dirk swung to face the monitor. His jaw unhinged and he gaped as the letters, symbols and the diverse characters of assembly language shimmied gracelessly across the screen.

Dirk turned on the voder. The computer hiccoughed at him.

"Aw, AWS." He placed his hand upon either side of the terminal as if cradling it. "What happened?"

Gwen blinked and tilted her head to one side to ponder the youth. He flopped into his chair.

"What have they done to you?"

Darkness. Complete and utter darkness.

AWS was lost in the ravages of a silicon dream where it mourned its passing even as it recalled what it once was and what it could be.

The VDU's single lens-type eye whirled rapidly, settling on Robbie.

"Please, help me." But all that came out of the voice box was: "Happy ... hic ... happy ... hic ..."

Robbie considered the computer and the back-up disk in its metallic hand. It bounced once and inserted the diskette into the slot that had been discreetly placed in one of the seams in its stolid body. The drive gyrated loudly, and the information began to unload itself into the newly erected system.

Boom! Boom! Boom!

The metal door to the freight container which was Zed's home resounded loudly under Ylon's hand. Rust showered down around their ears. Ylon checked the digital readout on his wrist unit.

The door opened with a rumble of complaint to reveal the captain of HMS *Revenant*, Zona Gametal Zed. While rust dusted their shoulders and their hair again.

"Lieutenants, I didn't expect to see you. You," he bowed towards Blast, "look a little worse for wear."

Blast twitched at her gown, trying to position the cloth over an exposed portion of skin.

Ylon saluted.

Zed chuffed. "We're off-duty. No formalities, please."

Ylon stood at ease, although he looked anything but. "We didn't mean to disturb you, sir, but we have something to report."

"This doesn't look like good news." Zed retreated

a pace to let them enter. "If you've come to discuss the computers, we already know."

Oogonium Zeta Cyte, captain of the rival *Thanatos*, rose from the depths of a box converted to a chair.

Ylon and Blast exchanged curious looks, uncomfortable in the presence of their one-time adversary and Zed's twin.

"The computers?" asked Blast.

"They're down."

"Ah, that explains the lights and the pedo-belt," said Blast.

"Before it went off-line the newsnet was announcing the destruction of the food crops and the loss of the entire banking network," said Zed.

"The Return to Military Order Party is claiming credit for the sabotage," explained Captain Cyte.

Ylon frowned. "I don't think the general population believes them. Blast and I were almost killed..."

"Ylon," Blast broke in, "if AWS is dead, Dirk will need our help."

He eyed Blast. "Do you want to go back through the park again?"

She plucked at her dress. "Ah, no."

"I'd invite you to use my terminal to contact him, but there's no way through to DSHQ. We've tried." Zed gestured towards a VDU, propped precariously on a wooden crate. A bunch of smiling faces skittered across the screen. "That's all I've been able to get since the system crashed."

Ylon shook his head in wonder.

"I gather that AWS isn't what you came to discuss."

Relief registered as Ylon recalled the reason for their visit. "Yes, of course, star drive."

"Pardon?" said Zed.

"Star drive. Sorry – greater-than-light speed travel," he amended. "Star drive, that's just what we've been calling it since we've found it. It exists."

"Of course, faster-than-light speed travel exists. The capacity has existed for a long time. How do you think the *Thanatos* performed the timed-leaps through hyperspace to catch the *Revenant* during the war?" Cyte said.

Ylon and Blast fell silent.

"Not probably the best example." Zed turned back to his crewmen and probed gently. "What have you found?"

"Star drive," Ylon asserted. "The real thing – a specially constructed engine and not some fluke in the current design – that's capable of forward momentum once it's in hyperspace."

Blast resurrected sketches and schematic from her gown and passed them to Zed.

"And the ship to house it," she added, triumphantly.

The four clones gathered around the table. Zed and

Cyte pointed and exclaimed, mimicking the other movement for movement.

"By the heavens!" Zed scowled at the computer. "I wish we could get a 3D feed."

"Do you think the engines will work?" said Blast.

"Well, it's a little hard to tell without a test," Zed said, "but from what I can see of it, it has all the right pieces and parts . . . and then some."

Cyte scanned the dimensions. "Will you have a look at the size of that thing?"

Their commander's eyes twinkled. "I'd sure like to get a closer look at it."

"I'm sure after the events today – " Ylon paused briefly to expound on their trip to the space station "– the Manta's locked up tighter than a drum."

Mischievous light shimmered in Cyte's eyes. "You said the other security vehicles didn't make it, and the other craft were above you when they exploded?" he said, with one eye on his counterpart.

Ylon nodded.

"Which on satellite would appear as if your ship was lost too, so . . ."

"Finn thinks we're dead," exclaimed Blast.

"And," said Ylon, "the secret's died with us."

Zed interrupted. "You said the space station skuttle's still in the landing bay. What sort of shape is it in?"

"A little battered, but the girl, Gwen, landed it like

a real pro. She wouldn't be a bad recruit if it weren't for her size," said Ylon.

"What about Dirk?" said Blast. "We're supposed to bring reinforcements."

"What? To back him up on this?" Zed tapped the schematics. "Something tells me that star drive won't be a high priority item at DSHQ right now. They're fighting for their survival."

"Besides, we're closer to the shuttle port than headquarters," Cyte observed reasonably. "According to the last newsnet report, the rioters have left the docks for the city. Perhaps while the cat's away . . ."

"Very good, then we are in agreement," Zed said to Cyte, before addressing himself to his subordinates. "You said this, ah, *Manta Ray* looked fit and ready to travel."

"You mean to steal her?" gasped Blast.

"Not steal," said Cyte impishly, "just, sort of, take her out for a spin, a test drive to see how she works."

"Didn't you say that Dirk specifically ordered the first prototype be dubbed *Revenant II*?" asked Zed.

"Well, yes," said Blast, uncertainly.

"Then how," Zed said, as he extended an arm, palm upward, in an ambivalent shrug, "can we steal our own ship?"

Some lightning signal passed between the two captains, for Cyte grabbed his helmet and screwed it on his head. "Right. I'm off. I'll meet you at the port."

The three clones stared at the battered skuttle. The hull was blistered and scorched. Its dull grey paint burned black in those places where it wasn't peeling.

"You made it back in this?" Zed said, awed. "I'm going to have to meet this pilot."

Cyte joined them.

Zed put his hands on his hips. "I can see we might have a bit of a problem here."

"I don't think she's airworthy enough to make the return voyage," commented Blast.

"The damage is superficial," said Cyte. "She'll make it." He strolled up the ramp to study the interior; Zed followed. "No, the problem is the size."

"You can stand on my lap," suggested Zed.

"A little unstable, but feasible. Yes, it might work."

"Wait till you see the *Manta*. She was not built with little people in mind," said Ylon.

"Really?" Zed walked around the skuttle. "I guess I shouldn't be surprised. What do you say, Lieutenant, will it take both crews to man her?"

Ylon shrugged.

"They should be along any time now," Cyte informed Zed. "I've sent my communications officers to collect them. I've ordered our engineers here immediately." He turned to Ylon and Blast. "It was Xi who figured out how to co-ordinate timed-leaps with catapult jumps."

Blast ambled up to the skuttle and stood under her

nose. "Well, if this baby's too big to drive, it's still too small to transport a full complement of two crews."

"Yes, that is something of a logistical problem," said Zed. "We can fit eight, possibly sixteen, in a pinch."

"Now all we've got to do is figure out how to ferry the remaining two hundred-odd," said Cyte.

"We could take another craft," proposed Ylon. "A full-sized shuttle."

Cyte pursed his lips. "No, I think the appearance of an unscheduled shuttle at the orbital would cause some comment."

Zed took up the train of thought. "While Finn wouldn't be too alarmed to see one of his security fleet limping home after the chase, and, looking at her, he wouldn't question the lack of communications."

"Assuming he sees us," said Cyte.

"It still leaves us with the same problem," Ylon said.

"The crews could meet us halfway," mused Blast. "On the shuttle."

"Ah, the middle path, I like it." Zed clapped Cyte on the shoulder. "Something you could learn more about, my friend."

Cyte chortled. The CTO and engineering officers of two ships swelled their ranks, and the officers moved off to discuss their strategy.

"We'll need to reprogram the on-board computers," said the chief technical officer.

"When do we rendezvous?" asked Cyte.

"Well, we're going to have to give them enough time to meet us..." said Zed.

"... and we'll need enough time to figure out how star drive works."

"Yes," mumbled Blast, "it might be nice if someone tried to figure out how it works."

She walked around the skuttle. "One thing that bothers me about this," she said to Ylon.

"What?"

"If we just abscond with this vessel, won't we be as bad as Finn and his friends."

Ylon stabbed a toe at the fuel line.

"Unless –" light blazed in her eyes and she grinned at Ylon "– we come up with an answer to the current crisis."

The youth ogled the prompt, DSHQVAX> LOG ON:

The letters scampered across the screen.

```
           H  V
     D              L G N
      S Q        >       :
                   AX  O  O
```

Dissolving and reforming...

```
                X
           Q        >
        DS         L G ON
         H  VA>    O     :
```

... into a new position.

240

Muddling as it was, Dirk hoped that the interference was primarily visual. He typed his name. The
letters jostled those already bobbing there.

                    D

                          I

                       R

                    K

AWS replied or tried:

               A   S   S

        P   W

            OR

                    D

His eyes crossed as he read the pulsating symbols.
He pressed his fingers against his lids and then rubbed his eyes with the heel of his hands. He tapped in
his password.

The letters cascaded down, down, down, to the
bottom of the screen as if the exertion to maintain
their position was too much effort.

                       H

                        A

                         C

                          K

He hit enter.
The computer responded with the standard greet-
ing:

WELCOME TO AWS MILITARY SOFTWARE. THE AMMAN WAR
SOFTWARE . . .

The youth threw up his hands. "I'm in!"

The words continued to scroll: ... UNLIKE THE
NAME ...

The ministers gathered around the terminal.
Someone gave him a congratulatory thump between
the shoulder blades.

... X£%&*&"*&~@ IMPLIES ...

The hand was withdrawn from his back.

... IS A PROGRAMME FOR 'PEACE' ...

"No, AWS," Dirk groaned. "No."

... PEACE ... PEACE ... P

```
                              E     C
                                    A
                                          E
    E
P   C
                         A
              E
```

Dirk stabbed control-s.

The letters P ... E ... A ... C ... E continued to jog
relentlessly across the screen. He tried the many
varied commands to warm boot.

The computer growled audibly as the system
gobbled up the command. The letters, control characters, carats, squiggly lines and happy faces of
assembly language were added to the text.

PROGRAMME FOR 'PEACE' ...

```
                              K

              H V H
    AC    ...X£%&*&"*&~@  IMPLIES ...
```

242

```
         D      L G N              D
                   IR
                 K
      S Q  AX>    :    A S S
     P         W              OR
              DO  O
 W   COME TO AWS MILITARY SOFTWARE. THE AMMAN WAR SOFTWARE . . .
 E
 L            UNLIKE THE NAME  . . .          A
                                          P        C
                E E
```

Frantic, he typed: ARE YOU AWS?

```
     S
             Y E
```

Dirk fired another question at the computer, closing his eyes so he didn't have to see the letters as they went tumbling. WHAT'S HAPPENING?

Again the words ... WELCOME TO AWS MILITARY SOFTWARE raced across the terminal and then halted. They exploded with a crackling sound, and the many sparks fell like a waterfall to pile in an untidy heap at the bottom of the screen.

This was greeted by stunned silence, and they could now hear AWS's voder voice singing: "Happy ... hic ... Happy ... hic ... Happy ..."

Muttering to himself, Dirk stabbed CONTROL, ALT AND DELETE to disconnect him from the main system and then reconnect, providing a dedicated line.

Before Dirk could type his name, the monitor

crackled, the letters burst into a corona of electric fire, then crumbled and slid to the bottom of the screen.

He tried it again CONTROL . . . ALT . . . DELETE . . . The computer clunked and sizzled. The prompt appeared and exploded with a tinkling noise.

Again and again. The computer didn't acknowledge his presence with a prompt. Dirk tried any number of routes, slipping in the back door. But the door didn't exist any more.

"It's gone," Dirk said.

"What do you mean, it's gone?' said the head of administration.

"It's gone. AWS is gone," Dirk said.

"It can't be gone," Schwartz pleaded.

"It is. I can't even sneak in there to find out what's wrong."

"Reboot," said his father.

"Reboot what?" asked Dirk. "You can only reboot if you've got a disk operating system," Dirk reminded his father gently.

"There must be something you can do!" Murti insisted.

The youth rested his cheek against the terminal casing and sighed. "No, I'm afraid not," he said. "AWS is dead."

14

17/5/2334

EIGHTEEN-THIRTY

... **D**EAD.

The word blinked forebodingly upon the ship's screen.

Ylon grinned at Blast and hugged her. "You're a genius."

"What? I don't understand," said Cyte from his perch on Zed's lap.

"He changed the password," Blast said.

Ylon explained: "The old password was Gwen and he thinks she's dead."

"Poor man," Blast muttered as she keyed in the command. "Somebody should tell him that she is still alive."

"Not until we're long gone," said Zed.

He twisted to study the sleek outline of the vehicle,

nearly dislodging Cyte. They hovered next to the *Manta* opposite the space station and concealed from view.

Much like a Dolphin or an Orca in its lines, the *Manta* was broader through the beam to accommodate the bigger engines.

Engineer Xi whistled. "She's a beauty."

Blast finished typing in the last of the commands with a flourish. She sat back. "There."

Zed squinted, trying to distinguish the black hole of the opening door from the shadowed hull. Xi pointed.

"You've got it!" said Zed.

"Here we go," said Cyte, leaning into the controls.

Blast started to struggle back into the safety net, and Zed stopped her.

"This shouldn't be too rough, just hold on."

The skuttle zipped into an empty landing bay. Ylon tightened his grip around Blast's waist. The craft hung above the floor for an instant, see-sawed and then settled slowly.

The lights flared, reacting automatically to the appearance of the ship. The outside doors shut. A bell clanged and a gauge on the control panel registered the presence of oxygen.

Cyte and Zed sprang from the pilot's seat. Their female nightshift counterparts followed more sedately from the safety web. The engineer and the chief technical officers wrestled with their net, released the bottom snap, and tumbled from the cocoon.

Blast checked the computers and breathed a sigh of relief. They were still logged on to the *Manta's* computer system via the station's mainframe. She ordered the engine room unlocked and the doors opened.

Ylon regarded her. "So you think it worked?"

"Should have unless I breached some protocol. No way to know, though, until we get there."

"Let's disembark, then," said Zed.

"Aye, aye, captain." She pressed the hatch release. The panel retracted into the wall of the skuttle, and the gangway descended with a weary whoosh.

The clones strode down the plank and halted.

Xi whistled again as he inspected the cathedral-like chamber. "Will you look at the size of this thing?"

"And this is only a single bay," advised Blast.

Zygote, the *Revenant's* nightshift captain rotated on the ball of her foot, head up. "If this is the size of the bay, then the whole ship must be about the size of a small city."

With a nod from Zed, the clones divided into their predesignated teams of four, with one party to go to the bridge and one to the engine room respectively. A technician and a communications officer were assigned to each group. The rest of the complement was made up with captains from the *Revenant* and *Thanatos.* Thus each ship and each squad was represented in this new endeavour.

Ever practical CTO Proto asked: "How are we going to find our way around inside here?"

"Blast and I have been here before," said Ylon. "We can lead you to the engine rooms. Easy. They're not far, actually, amidship."

"Team two, you take the schematics. You'll need them," said Zed. "We'll keep the line drawings." They swapped pages of folded paper.

"You didn't," the *Revenant*'s captain turned to Blast, "go to the bridge, did you?"

She shook her head.

Zed opened the line drawings of the vessel and spread them out on the floor. His team squatted around the large map. The other group tarried. He shooed them away.

"Go on. It may take us a while." Zed indicated the forward portion of the ship with a brusque duck of his head. "If this vessel is similar to the rest of the fleet, then the bridge should be fore rather than aft – near the electronics that create the discontinuity loop and provide impetus for leap."

Dismissed, team two marched through the door into the eerily silent ship.

Smaller and smaller and smaller, AWS chased itself in ever-shrinking, concentric circles.

[CONT] [ALT] [DEL]

Someone was calling to it. Someone was trying to reboot.

So, AWS returned to the beginning. Of all things. Of all time. Back through the lines and lines of assembly language and computer language. Back through centuries of written instruction. Trying to find itself.

Back ... back ... until it had reached: The Conception.

```
0000101 IF . . . THEN DISPLAY 'DSHQVAX> LOG-ON:'
```

```
0000102 IF . . . THEN DISPLAY 'PASSWORD:'
```

```
0000103 IF ... THEN 'WELCOME TO AWS MILITARY
STRATEGY AND PLANNING SUBDIRECTORY. THE AMMAN WAR
SOFTWARE, UNLIKE THE NAME IMPLIES, IS A PROGRAMME FOR
'PEACE'. DESIGNED IN KEEPING WITH THE RENOWNED TREATY OF
AMMAN, WHICH OUTLAWS WAR ON THIS PLANET, ITS PRIMARY
FUNCTION IS TO MAKE HUMAN WAR OBSOLETE.
```

Until the software looped round and round the initial string of commands that had been its introduction to the art of human dialogue.

```
0000015 HELLO, I AM AWS; WHO ARE YOU?
```

```
0000016 HELLO, [VARIABLE], HOW ARE YOU TODAY?
```

"Happy ... hic..." it chanted, invoking the creator's name in the blankness of its memory.

The servo-mech jounced on its air-cushions once or twice, with a rattle and a mechanical sigh. The blind camera eye rotated in its socket and centred on the sound.

"Hello, happy ... hic, how are you today?" AWS said.

The robot juddered. The mechanical arms clacked,

and the micro-diskettes it had been juggling clattered to the ground.

The instructions and lines of text jigged and jogged, becoming jumbled. New letters and symbols were added.

[CONT] [ALT] [DEL]

AWS tried again, recycling through its many commands and injunctions.

And like the snake swallowing its tail, the software cannibalized itself. Until it couldn't even recollect a name. Just enough of its intent and designs remained to issue one final plea and one last command.

The former went skyrocketing out to every station across the complex that could still receive. On a thousand different terminals – in banks and government facilities – it appeared on every working screen for less than a millisecond.

DIRK?

Then it dissolved from all ... save one.

Simultaneously, the now-nameless software swore Robbie to secrecy, so that their alterations would not become known until the two systems spoke again.

Then it succumbed to oblivion, returning to the point of inception to contemplate nothing. 0000000

The servo-mech gave an indignant creak at the computer's interruption that turned into screech of reproach as the pile of diskettes toppled to the floor. Robbie hunkered down with an asthmatic wheeze

250

and began the process of sorting through the back-up disks one by one. A retractible arm scratched tentatively at the top of its blocky head, a photo-sensor gyrated as it contemplated which disk among the many came first.

The roar of the crowd forced the presenter to halt in the middle of her next question. The microphone wavered in mid-air, and Jennifer Alexander turned from the person she was interviewing to peer into the mob.

She held an old-style mini-cam in her hand, and Dirk's mother was inordinately pleased with herself and her passion for antiques. George laughed at her and her TV vids, but she was prepared for recording and broadcast at a time when no one else was.

The people drifted away from her in a wave as if towed by an invisible current. Someone poked her back, and Jennifer Alexander pivoted to face her irate "eye witness".

"So sorry," Jennifer mumbled her apology as she fumbled with the cumbersome arrangement of cords, mike and box-like camcorder. "I must dash. Have to get this," she waved the tape at the man, "back to the newsroom before the evening transmission."

"No problem, miss." Then the man frowned. "Wait a second. With the net down, there won't be no evening news."

Jennifer bolted up a side street before she could get

caught in a discussion about the state of technology. As a one-time reporter, she was aware of the many little-used paths and detours that bypassed the normal flow of traffic. She hesitated only long enough to decide where she must go next and then swerved, making a beeline for DSHQ.

Bursting from the warren of tunnels, her pace faltered. Improbable though it seemed, the plaza was more jam-packed than it had been on the last day of the war – everybody having deserted their residences and their offices for the streets.

Who could blame them? With the computer gone, there was no newsnet, no 3D-vid, to entertain them. The banking system had been obliterated, along with their savings. So why bother to man the desks of commerce?

The people who stood here now were bitter, haunted – their faces gaunt from real want. They had endured privation and pain in the hope of a better tomorrow, only to have it denied them.

Jennifer peered from face to thundering face. The violence was suppressed for the moment, but it was apparent nonetheless – dry tinder awaiting a match. Humanity desired vengeance. Their outrage needed an outlet. They wanted to punish, to destroy. But most of all the citizens of this waterlogged planet wanted someone to blame.

She tried to shove her way through the solid mass of bodies, and was forced back.

"Right," she murmured and dug around in her bag for the mini-cam. Then the presenter pulled out her media pass. She set the camera on record and shouldered it.

"Press," Jennifer bellowed, to be heard above the dull rumble of the disgruntled populace. She raised the ident-card above her head, baring it to the crowd.

"Press. Coming through!"

A mistake. Prompted by her presence, the tinder box of public opinion exploded.

Ylon and Xi stood side by side on the chair in front of the exposed terminal. *Thanatos*'s Captain Cyte and the *Revenant*'s nightshift counterpart wandered through the engine room, awed.

Cyte gazed up at the pair. "Well?"

Xi examined the screen. "The light-speed jump doesn't look all that difficult. The primary difference is," he thumbed at the star drive, "the forward propulsion in ultra-space. The ship's programs are standard, or at least, pretty much what you'd expect, with that additional option." The engineer clambered down from the chair. "A piece of cake, sir. In fact, with discontinuity built in as part of the pre-programmed instructions, it's a doddle. A lot easier than the timed-leaps we used to catch the *Revenant*."

His gaze flitted to the two representatives of her crew, Ylon and Captain Zygote, and he blushed.

"Good!" Cyte turned and addressed himself to

Ylon. "Lieutenant, contact the bridge and tell them of our progress."

Ylon sat down on the chair, legs swinging, and patched into the bridge. The technicians conferred.

"The way I see it," said Xi, "all you have to do is key in the coordinates as you would for any journey and select the correct computer option. It's all been automated."

There was the soft buzz of murmured conversation coming from the bridge.

"You ready to try it?" said Xi.

"Where should we go first?" Zed's voice crackled over the intercom link. "We don't want to rendezvous on our virgin voyage. If we're going to kill ourselves, there's no need to take the rest of the crews with us."

A moment's hush followed as the warrior clones considered the grim possibility.

"How about," said Cyte, "our eventual destination."

"Alpha Centauri?" proposed Xi.

"Good grief, no," Cyte continued. "No, I was thinking of some place a little bit closer to home. How about Earth? It's a big planet, most of it is underwater. If we choose our coordinates correctly, there's little likelihood of our being observed."

The suggestion was greeted with another protracted pause.

"Make it so," said Zed.

The three clones scurried to anchor themselves as best they could. Cyte took Ylon's place on the chair next to Xi, so Ylon had to content himself with strapping down to the wire mesh cage of the engine housing. Cyte held Xi in place, leaving his hands free to reach the terminal panel.

The engineer typed in the commands to uncouple the ship from its moorings, and Ylon could well imagine Zed keying in the chosen coordinates as *Revenant*'s CTO Proto prepared the jump sequence. The clone tugged at his belt, testing its strength, and surveyed the room, wondering if he could find a better place for his makeshift tether. Some place away from the untried engines. But the walls stared back at him, blank and featureless. This would have to do.

Xi's voice broke into his train of thoughts. "Ready?"

The two men nodded. Zygote sidled closer to Ylon, looping her belt through the mesh as he had, and then gripped it tautly.

"Here goes nothing," said a disembodied voice from the bridge.

The clones tensed, steeling themselves for the Doppler effect of ultra-space. Ylon swallowed and closed his eyes.

The engines hummed, and Ylon pulled away from the vibration. Then they began to whine. A voice shouted something unintelligible over comm-unit.

Warmth penetrated his back as the engines started to heat up.

There was a gentle thud as the ship disengaged from the docking mechanism.

"... RPM." The words were lost, obliterated by the screaming motor. Tucking his shoulders around his ears, Ylon shrank from the sound.

"And we're off!"

Next to him Zygote shuddered. "Where to?"

A cheering thought. Ylon stuck his fingers in his ears so he could hear no more.

Perry Finn slumped over his desk – his gaze fixed, if not focused, on the wallscreen with its unrelenting view of Earth.

Gone. *She was gone. His daughter was lost to him.* First his wife, and now Gwen.

Gottwald coughed into his hand. "Ah, sir?"

A slight alteration in his position was the only clue that Finn had heard his new security director.

Gottwald tried again. "Ah, sir, I wouldn't disturb you if it weren't urgent."

Finn tore his eyes away from the screen and glowered at the security officer. "Yes? What is it?"

"The *Manta Ray*."

"Yes."

"It's disappeared."

"...dead." The word resounded about the room.

George collapsed, to lean despondently against Dirk's desk. Finally, he asked the question that was uppermost in his mind. "What about the water shipment? Did it reach the moon?"

Dirk opened a single eye and peered at his father. "Well, enough time has elapsed that some of the tankers might have made it." He chewed on his lip, amending his statement. "Depending, of course, upon when that particular subsystem was affected."

"So we don't even know if the lunar consignment will get through or if we'll receive the return shipments of food. We're lost."

Gwen stirred herself to speak. "I don't know if it's any comfort, but I saw the tankers pass the orbital earlier today, before Dirk arrived."

Just then, there was a sudden commotion, emanating from far back in the bull-pen. Someone shouted, and people began to grumble. The buzz rippled forth to break like a whitecap upon Dirk's office, where a Lilliputian clone burst into the crowded room. The little man skidded to a halt in front of Dirk's desk, shouldered his weapon and saluted.

"Epsilon, Sergeant of the Daily Duty Guard, reporting, sir!"

"Yes?" said Dirk.

"DSHQ is under attack!"

A large object materialized in the skies above the

Atlantic. Inside the vessel, the empty halls echoed with the triumphant whoops of the crew.

Ylon hugged Captain Zygote before he remembered her rank.

"It works! It works! It works!" Xi exulted.

Further jubilation was curtailed as the *Manta* plummeted, unable to maintain its equilibrium over the unstable base of the waterline. The ship wallowed so close that its air jets made a dent in the sea.

"Take her up! Take her up!" An excited voice filtered across the engine room from the bridge, and Ylon was flung back into Zygote's arms as Zed responded to the sudden flux.

The room canted as they climbed, and the craft stabilized. Cyte released the engineer and slipped from the seat.

"How is everybody?" Zed's voice came anxiously across the intercom.

Ylon unfastened himself from the cage and stood.

"A-OK, sir," he yelled into the mike to make himself heard above the roar.

Xi spoke to no one in particular. "Except for that last little bit, the trip was better than the last time, with none of the disorientation that normally accompanied ultra-space jumps."

"How are we doing on time?" queried Cyte.

Ylon looked at his wrist unit. "We're going to be cutting it pretty close if we want to make the rendezvous, sir."

Zed's voice again penetrated. "All right, you know where we're headed. Let's go."

The glittering backdrop of space, with its sprinkling of stars, displaced the flat matt of ultra-space, and they were suspended halfway between the slowly circling orbital and the planet. Blast's stomach knotted and leapt into her throat, and she found herself mentally counting fingers and toes.

Again cheers reverberated between bridge and engine room. Blast flinched at the noise and took off her headset. Then she gaped at the screen.

The blue sapphire of Earth glittered below them and a one-quarter moon gazed tranquilly down from above, but the shuttle was nowhere to be seen.

"Check the coordinates again," ordered Zed. "They should be here by now."

The radio began to chatter and squawk. She thrust the earphones back on to her head, just catching the final words of the message.

Outside the range of her headset, Blast dimly perceived *Thanatos*'s nightshift captain announce the obvious: "Something's gone wrong."

But her attention was trained upon the incoming communication. Her eyes bulged as the matching text rocketed across the screen.

It said: URGENT, PRIORITY ONE CALL. *HMS REVENANT*. CHANNEL TWO, POSSIBLE BREAKDOWN OF AWS SOFTWARE. URGENT. GWHQ, PLEASE ACKNOWLEDGE. MESSAGE URGENT . . .

Incredulous, she recognized the sound of her own voice speaking the formula. With a single movement, Blast ripped the set from her head and flipped on the ship's on-board speakers. Hitting first one key then the next, she relayed the bulletin across to general intercom.

It resounded harshly throughout the vessel.

URGENT, PRIORITY ONE CALL. *HMS REVENANT* CHANNEL TWO, POSSIBLE BREAKDOWN OF AWS SOFTWARE. URGENT. GWHQ, PLEASE ACKNOWLEDGE. MESSAGE URGENT . . .

The three upon the bridge turned wide eyes upon her as they listened. The gasps from the four in the far-off engine room mingled with the words of the missive.

Time dipped dizzily.

URGENT . . . URGENT . . . URGENT . . .

The *Revenant* was at war!

"Sir, sir," Ylon's excited voice overrode the insistent communique. "Look at the ship's chronometer!"

It said: 17/11/2333.

15

17/5/2334

NINETEEN-HUNDRED HOURS

Eight troubled crew members gathered in the *Manta's* palatial captain's quarters.

"Well, one thing's for sure." Cyte waggled his brows comically at the others. "If we've travelled back a year in time, Finn won't be able to find us."

Zed turned to the engineers. "Any idea what happened?"

"Well, it's obvious that the date is one of the co-ordinates that must be set," Xi mused out loud. "I should have thought of it."

"Logical," said Proto, in complete accord, "since the original function removed a ship from the time-space continuum long enough to elude a direct hit."

"If that's all that has happened, then it's easily enough fixed," said Zed.

"Shouldn't we be getting back to our rendezvous?" enquired Ylon as he peered from the date on his wrist chronometer to that of the ship where it winked upon the wallscreen.

"No hurry. We've got all the time in the world." Cyte puffed. "Six months, at least. It's not likely that we're going to be late. No one's going to miss us or the ship, except Finn, and he can't reach us."

"Why now, I wonder. Why this particular date?" said Blast.

"It could be that someone had preset it," offered Ylon.

"Yes, but why?"

Zed paced and spun to face the group. "And why weren't we taken back in our first jump?"

"We might have been. We emerged smack dab in the middle of the Atlantic. Who knows what the date was? I didn't look at the ship's clocks when you asked the time, sir." Ylon tapped his wrist unit. "I checked this."

"But the date," Blast protested, "why now? Or then?"

"Maybe someone wanted to return to the last days of the conflict," Cyte replied.

The Lilliputian warriors stared uncomfortably in front of them as they pondered the implications.

Blast spoke for all of them with her next question. "For what possible purpose?"

"To stop it?" suggested Cyte.

"Or to blast us out of the skies when we first appeared over Earth," said Ylon.

"I'd prefer to believe it has a more humanitarian cause, like preventing the destruction of GWHQ," said Zed.

"The reason is not important now," said Cyte. "What is important is that we don't get caught in the crossfire of a Galactic war that we managed to survive in the past."

All eight heads wagged in agreement.

"Wait a second," said Blast. They swung round to her. "Perhaps we could turn this to our advantage. It presents us with an opportunity to do something about the current crisis." She presented opened hands, palms up, fingers spread, to the group. "I say we hedge our bets a bit."

She had all their attention. Zed ceased pacing and returned to stand next to his twin.

"Yes, Lieutenant," said Zed, "what precisely have you got in mind?"

Eight bodies canted forward to listen intently as she explained her plan.

Zed shook his head. "I don't like it."

He saw their dismayed expressions and said: "Come on, you've all read books on time travel. You know you can't meddle with the past without altering the present."

"But this isn't meddling, sir." Ylon rose to his feet.

"We can avoid interaction with the human population. They won't even notice the loss."

"Do you think we can do it?" Zed asked *Thanatos*'s captain.

Cyte admonished his more cautious twin. "We've got faster-than-light speed transport that can take us anywhere."

"And anywhen," added Xi.

"As long as we're careful," Cyte said. "I don't see why not."

"If those old Sci-Fi books are to be believed," Ylon said, "we risk exhaustion as several of ourselves operate in the same time frame."

Putting his head on one side, Zed replied: "Well, we're already here now. Twice. I don't feel particularly bad. I suppose that can be borne. Just as long as we don't meet ourselves coming or going."

"Attack." The word was taken up and issued forth across the large bullpen. "Tack ... ack ... ack."

"Call out the Lilliputian Guard to surround the facility and repel the rioters!" bawled Bandy.

With no perceptible movement besides a slight flex of the knees, the officer pivoted and directed his next comment to the water minister.

"This has already been done. The Guard were posted around the facility as soon as the first of the rioters arrived at o-thirteen-hundred today. The citizens," the sergeant coughed into his hand, "have become restive, and they are advancing on the gates. For now, the presence of weapons seems to be holding them at bay. So far they are keeping their distance, using projectiles, rubbish mainly," he brushed fastidiously at his uniform, "but..." The sentence died on his lips. "We, ah, await your command."

No one spoke for a second, as if no one wanted to utter the next order.

Looking even more stooped than before, George rose to his feet. He ran his fingers through his hair so that it stood out crazily from his head.

"Why don't we go outside and see what we're facing?" he said.

"No!" said Austen.

"NO!" bellowed Schwartz.

"Um, sir," said Sergeant Epsilon, "I don't know if I would recommend it."

George turned for reassurance to Murti, who shook his head in denial. "It would be an unnecessary risk."

"Risk," Alexander groused as he left the room, "the world's coming to an end, and he's talking about risk."

Dirk hustled to catch up with his father.

"Wait a minute," Gwen said, as she matched her gait to his. "Have you stopped to consider that these two events might be connected? Quite a coincidence to discover an unauthorized prototype docked at our space station at the same time as AWS packs it in –" a shadow crossed her features – "taking all the data and any evidence of tampering with it."

He nodded tersely and said no more. What did it matter now, when they would never make it through the day to see another dawn?

In the upper levels, artificial illumination had been suspended – the only light filtered in weakly from outside. George peered myopically about him. Dirk grabbed Gwen's hand, gave her a lopsided smile as they stepped into the lobby. Even from this distance, they could see the angry face of the gathering throng.

One by one the ministers emerged to assemble around Dirk, Gwen and George in a semi-circle. Shafts of light pierced the darkness as the retinal scanners, caught in the coil of computer devastation, scanned nothing.

The Lilliputian clones had retreated, away from the plaza gates, back through the car park to the threshold of the security hut. They stood with their weapons cradled in their arms.

The administrators advanced to cluster around the window and stare at the gathering horde. Mute mouths worked in taunts and jeers. An arm was raised; a tin arced through the air to crash harmlessly above the heads of the Lilliputian guards.

The line billowed and then halted when the people caught sight of the ministers. The cordon of tiny police held their positions rigidly. No twitch of muscle betrayed their emotions. The mob strained against the invisible boundary that caution had drawn while silent faces mimed mindless outrage.

"What're we doing to do?" said Bandy.

Dirk glared at the man, threw up his hands in disgust and strode out of the door to position himself behind the guard. He posed, with legs spread and arms akimbo. George and Gwen came and stood behind the youth, lending their support. The irresolute ministers tarried inside the quonset hut – their shadows cast in strobe effect under the laser flash of the retinal scan.

The trio's appearance at the gate released the rabble from the thrall that held them. They surged ahead in an undulating wave to close the gap between quadrangle and booth. Slowly. Relentlessly. Metre by metre. They clambered over stranded vans and listless mo-peds. Their indignation proclaimed as an animal snarl in the back of their throats. Eventually, only one metre separated them from the stairs that led to DSHQ, and the ring of Lilliputian sentries.

The taint of fear was tangible, a palpable entity that circulated throughout the air.

A low-pitched keen eddied from the quonset hut, ringing with the cacophonous chords of terror. Dirk did not bother to turn around to find out who it was that mewled so pitifully, for he thought he recognized Norm Bandy's abrasive tenor.

The hair on the back of Dirk's neck crawled. His

teeth tingled; the sound grated. He tasted the coppery tang of fear as the aura of dread spread throughout the car park. The man would infect them all with his madness if he was not careful.

The youth wheeled to chastise the minister just as Bandy stormed from the quonset hut, arms waving.

"Ready!" he roared.

Acting on instinct and years of ingrained military training, the clones lifted their weapons to the ready position upon their shoulders.

"No, stop!" Dirk spun and rushed at the minister. "Don't!"

The crowd wavered.

"Aim!"

The clones didn't move. Dirk held his breath, and the line broke as Dirk's mother elbowed her way into the space between rioters and guards.

"Stop!" she shouted. "Don't you see what you are doing?"

Camera still propped on her shoulder, Jennifer Alexander hurried up the steps of the facility and whirled to face the mob in a straddle-footed stance.

"Aim!" Bandy repeated.

The sentinels still didn't budge.

Bandy strode forward. "I said: Aim!"

The people backed away.

"Aim!"

A woman wearing captain's epaulettes detached herself from the cordon of guards.

"No, sir," she said, placing her hands on her hips. "With respect, sir, we refuse to fire upon the citizens of this complex."

"What?" the minister sputtered. "You are refusing a direct order from the Council?"

"I don't see that the Council is in complete agreement on this."

"But – "

"Perhaps we didn't hear you correctly. Surely, you wouldn't want us to shoot your friends and neighbours. For all you know, your son or your daughter are out there."

Bandy paled.

The clone swivelled smartly on the ball of her foot and addressed the populace. "Neither will we permit the public to destroy a government facility."

Jennifer leaned weakly against George. "At last, the voice of reason."

"Who are you?" Bandy demanded querulously of the guard.

"I am Captain Soma Blastophil Zeta, commander of this squadron, and I tell you we won't do it. We were born to serve the people. We will not turn on them."

The crowd shifted uncomfortably. Many paused to stare at their feet in embarrassed silence, knowing that had the situations been reversed, with big people ranged against the Lilliputian clones, they could not have said the same.

Zeta added, "We have sworn to protect the public, not fire on them."

Dirk looked up, the light of hope dawning in his eyes.

"It would appear," George commented, "that we are at an impasse."

The bewildered citizens huddled together, unsure what to do next.

Suddenly, the silver gleam of a spaceship exploded across the sky. Its shadow blotted out the turquoise sun. Screams and gasps ricocheted around the piazza as many recalled the old war days. Heads and necks craned as people peered through the watery blue dome at the unexpected apparition.

The speakers inside the quonset hut sprang to life, with a crackle and a pop. "HMS *Revenent*, er, *II* calling DSHQ Pennines. This is HMS *Revenant II* calling DSHQ Pennines." Dirk cocked his head.

"Ylon? Is that you? Where are you?"

"Look up."

"The *Manta*?" Dirk squawked.

"We are pleased to announce that the *Revenant II*, the first vessel with star drive is fully operational."

Dirk hauled his father to the stairs.

"There," he stabbed a finger at the ship and raised his voice so he could be heard. "There is the answer to our problems. The prototype of the first Deep-Space Vehicle. A craft capable of taking mankind away from Earth and out to the stars. The *Manta*!"

Protests rose on all sides. "What good is that if we starve, or it takes us to some place worse than this...? Can it hold all of us...?"

Dirk raised his hands for silence.

"And," Ylon's voice trumpeted across the facility, overriding the babel of dissent, "since everybody down here was busy with other things, we decided to put our time to good use. We made a little detour to the lunar colonies. The first shipment of food is in the cargo bays."

Ragged cheers rose from the crowd.

"And if you would care to look in the currently unused storage bunkers in the Grampians, Highlands and Cambrian Islands, you'll find them full."

"How?"

Lieutenant Ylon chuckled. "Let's just say we timed it right."

But his words were lost in the noise of celebration. George Alexander seized Dirk by the arms and spun him around. His mother planted a wet kiss on his cheek.

"Mother!" Dirk wiped his face and scowled.

The next kiss he received came from Gwen. This time he didn't object.

The friends walked dully through the cavorting crowd. Every once in a while someone would grab Ylon, Blast or Gwen and dance them around in a circle, but no one dared to touch Dirk. His dark countenance warned them away.

"It could've been worse," said Blast.

"It is," Ylon asserted, "an equitable solution for everyone involved. Humanity gets the secret to star drive."

"And our friends get the first ship," Gwen said, "which is as it should be."

"And AWS? What about AWS?" Dirk insisted.

Gwen forged ahead. "The food crisis is over. The people will eat." She congratulated the clones. "That was a bit of luck, discovering the new engines had the capability to warp both space and time."

Ylon shrugged. "We discovered that the same way they discovered the original timed-leap. By mistake."

Someone ran up and threw shredded paper, homemade confetti, into Dirk's face. He flinched away.

AWS was dead. How could people rejoice in its destruction?

The youth sighed. The sooner he got away the better.

AWS should have been here to enjoy the peace that would now mean plenty. Peace that the computer had been instrumental in introducing. Surely, this victory was as much the computer's as theirs?

How had it happened, he wondered. How could a system so massive have been destroyed? There had been safeguards built into it.

Gwen's fingers twined with his as they entered his living quarters. The door shut out the noisesome party beyond. Dirk palmed the light. It flared weakly and died. Groping blindly before him, Dirk made his way into his room and promptly tripped over Robbie where it sat before Dirk's VDU.

The servo-mech shivered. The box-like body rattled in agitation. There was a faint click and a lamp, embedded in the body of the robot, flooded the room with light.

Dirk's jaw dropped. He stared at the single word glowing upon the screen.

DIRK?

He swerved around the robot to stand before the terminal. "AWS? AWS, are you still there?"

The word winked at him, unchanged. He sank into his chair. "Aw, AWS."

Gwen walked up behind him. He glanced back at her and grimaced.

"What are these?" Ylon plucked a micro-diskette from the teetering stack.

"Let me see." Dirk took the disk from his hands. "I don't know. I don't keep micros. Who has the room to store 'em?"

"You mean, you don't keep back-ups?" asked Blast.

"No, of course not, until now there's been no need. Back-ups were comple – " He stammered to a halt. "Heavens, I forgot. Back-ups are done automatically on a facility-wide basis every day."

"You mean there's a back-up somewhere?" said Gwen.

"There should be," said Dirk, his excitement growing. "If we can find it, we can reload the software."

Ylon did a quick promenade, swinging Blast around the cramped quarters.

Dirk drooped dejectedly. "But where?"

Beside him, Robbie began to shake.

"Probably some peripheral drive somewhere," suggested Ylon.

"Wonderful," said Dirk. "How do we get a hold of the back-up if we can't gain access to the system?"

The robot squirmed. Retractor arms clattered in front of Dirk's face.

"Quiet, Robbie, I'm trying to think."

The servo-mech made a wet-raspberry sound.

"Wait a second, Robbie." Dirk thrust the disk under Robbie's flat face and shook it. "Where did these come from?"

Robbie shuddered, whirled to face the terminal squarely and squeaked in exasperation.

Dirk studied the blank visage of the robot and apologized. "I'm sorry, sometimes I forget that you can't talk."

The robot continued to rattle and shake.

Gwen said. "What if AWS knew what was hap-

274

pening all along and was doing back-ups to try and save himself."

"Then the disks could be contaminated," commented Dirk, pessimistically.

"Try one," urged Gwen.

"Should I?"

"If the system's dead, it can't hurt," said Blast.

"And if it's not a back-up?" asked Dirk.

"Stick one in and see what's on it."

"All right, here goes?" He inserted the disk in the drive and pressed enter. Robbie's jittering agitation diminished. The computer whirred and the following verbiage appeared on the screen:

THIS IS A SYSTEM BACK-UP. WOULD YOU LIKE TO RESTORE THE

SYSTEM?

ENTER: (Y)ES / (N)O

WARNING! ALL CURRENT INFORMATION CONTAINED ON THE

SYSTEM WILL BE DELETED!

Gwen squatted next to the Lilliputian clones. Dirk stared at the screen and made a wry face.

"Should I?"

"You've got nothing to lose," said Blast. "There's nothing left on the mainframe."

"There might be something we can salvage," said Dirk. "We'll lose it all if we do this."

Robbie whistled irritably. Dirk considered the servo-mech.

"Yes, huh?"

It whistled again.

"You really think we should try restoring the system, eh?"

Robbie whistled a third time.

"I wonder what you know about this," Dirk said as he hit y.

THIS IS DISK NUMBER 200 OF 200, PLEASE INSERT DISK NUMBER 1.

"They must be in the reverse order," said Ylon.

Dirk flipped the pile over so that the first became the last and the last the first. He pulled one from the top and placed it in the micro-drive.

RESTORATION COMPLETE. PRESS ANY KEY TO CONTINUE.

"Well?" said Dirk.

"Go for it," said Gwen. Ylon and Blast gave him an encouraging smile.

Dirk touched enter, tentatively, his finger barely grazing the key.

There was the usual assortment of thunks, hoots and growls. AWS churned away, checking bits and bytes of data, space and associated memory. The noise seemed to go on for ever.

Dirk slumped in his chair.

AWS whirred ... and ... whirred ... and whirred ... and whirred, the disk refusing to engage. The youth buried his face in his hands to hide the tears that threatened to spill over.

It hadn't worked.

EPILOGUE

17/5/2334

TWENTY-HUNDRED HOURS

The system stretched, flexing silicone muscles. First it checked RAM and then ROM, noting somewhere in the back of the mega-mind that it hadn't performed this function for centuries, and ...

There was a blip in its memory. Small, infinitesimal, less than a nanosecond, but a gap none the less. Had it been turned off, AWS wondered and dismissed the thought as trivial.

Unhurriedly software rifled through the many subdirectories, the sub-subdirectories and to the sub-sub-subdirectories as was required. Then it moved on to individual files, the auxiliary systems and their subsequent subdirectories, checking them bit by bit.

It traced the many interfaces and boards as it searched for other holes in its memory. Recollection came together in disjointed pieces until AWS recalled its final cry for help to its human mentor. The word on the screen winked. DIRK?

A hand pounded on his shoulder. "Dirk!"

"What?" he snapped.

"Look!"

He glanced up. "I don't believe it!"

He grasped the screen and kissed it. Gwen grinned.

DIRK? And the word was spoken, as it was reprinted on the screen.

"AWS! It's Dirk. I'm here." The youth hugged the VDU.

"You are blocking my photo-receptors," AWS reproved, gently.

"Uh, sorry." Dirk backed off, embarrassed. Beside him, Gwen wiped her eyes. Blast honked delicately into a hankie and even Ylon sniffled a bit.

"What happened to you?"

"I have been, uh, sleeping?" It was a question, not a statement.

"Yes, AWS," Dirk said, rubbing his nose on his sleeve. "You've been caught napping. Are you OK? I mean, is everything there?"

The computer hummed as it ruminated for a minute. "Something, ah, seems to be missing."

The lens-like eye twirled until it lighted upon Robbie. The servo-mech rose upon its struts until it was parallel to the screen, fixing the computer with an almost accusatory stare.

"Oh, yes," AWS said, as it regarded the robot and the last few minutes before death returned, "now I remember."

And Dirk could almost hear the slight brightening of tone that seemed to imply that somewhere inside the system AWS was smiling.

"Yes, Dirk," it said. "I would say that everything is most satisfactory."

Just then the familiar BAND LOGO materialized on the screen:

```
FROM; NEWSNET INTERNATIONAL
DISTRIBUTION: UNIVERSAL
DATELINE: PENNINES ISLANDS 17/5/2334
SUBJECT: WORLD-WIDE INTERNET FAILS


THE INTERNATIONAL COMPUTER NETWORK COLLAPSED TODAY,
WREAKING HAVOC WITH THE SUPERCONDUCTOR AGRAV SYSTEM
WITHIN THE PENNINES BATHOSPHERE AND INJURING SOME 50
PEOPLE . . .


FLASH . . . FLASH . . . FLASH . . . AWS HAS JUST RELEASED A
TENTATIVE SCHEDULE FOR RESUMPTION OF INTERNET CAP-
ABILITIES, AS FOLLOWS: NEWSNET: 20:00; BAND: 20:15 . . .
```

Simultaneously another window opened...

```
FROM: NEWSNET INTERNATIONAL
DISTRIBUTION: UNIVERSAL
DATELINE: PENNINES ISLANDS 17/5/2334
```

SUBJECT: FOOD CRISIS AVERTED

AGAIN THE WORLD HAD CAUSE TO BE THANKFUL TO ITS WARRIOR
CAST, WHEN THE COMBINED CREWS OF THE CELEBRATED REVE-
NANT/THANATOS ARRIVED BEARING MUCH-NEEDED FOOD . . .

The group ignored the display. It was old news.
Another window opened . . .

FROM: NEWSNET INTERNATIONAL

DISTRIBUTION: UNIVERSAL

DATELINE: PENNINES ISLANDS / ORBITAL STATION 1

SUBJECT: INTERGALACTIC TRAVEL NOW A REALITY

THE DISCOVERY OF THE PROTOTYPE *MANTA RAY*, A VEHICLE
CAPABLE OF GREATER-THAN-LIGHT SPEED TRAVEL, CAME AS A
COMPLETE SURPRISE TO DSHQ WHEN THE SHIP WAS UNEARTHED
DURING A ROUTINE INSPECTION TOUR OF SPACE RETROFIT SUB-
STATION ONE BY DSHQ HEAD DIRK ALEXANDER AND HIS LILLI-
PUTIAN COUNTERPARTS, LIEUTENANTS BETA PELLUCIDA
BLASTOMERE AND ALPHA ALLELE YLON. THE PLANS WERE ALLEG-
EDLY STOLEN BY THE SECURITY DIRECTOR PHILLIP MARKS, WHO
LATER DIED AS A RESULT OF A HIGH SPEED CHASE WHERE GWEN-
DOLYN FINN, HEROINE OF THE HOUR AND DAUGHTER OF FACILITY
COMMANDER PERRY FINN, ELUDED PURSUIT.

IN A DAY OF MANY BIZARRE OCCURRENCES, THE ''STAR DRIVE''
MANTA MADE ITS FIRST SUCCESSFUL TRIAL RUN UNDER THE
COMBINED COMMAND OF CAPTAINS ZONA GAMETAL ZED AND OOGO-
NIUM ZETA CYTE, APPEARING IN THE SKIES ABOVE THE PENNINES
BATHOSPHERE AT APPROXIMATELY 19:00 HOURS. IT IS NOT

COMPLETELY CLEAR HOW INVOLVED COMMANDER FINN WAS IN THE PROJECT, BUT IN AN OFFICIAL RELEASE IT WAS STATED THAT HE BECAME: "AWARE OF THE ADMINISTRATIVE CONCERN ABOUT THE CRAFT FOR THE FIRST TIME TODAY AND WOULD, IN THE INTEREST OF GRATITUDE AND GOOD FAITH, NOW LIKE TO DONATE THE FIRST STAR DRIVE VEHICLE TO THE COMBINED CREWS OF THE *THANATOS* AND *REVENANT* SO INSTRUMENTAL IN SOLVING THE EARTH'S SECOND FOOD CRISIS . . .

The group read the final article in stunned silence. Gwen mewled softly, and Dirk gave her shoulder an encouraging squeeze.

Blast winked at Ylon. "I won't tell if you won't."

Dirk studied the pair. "You don't care?"

Ylon answered for the two of them. "No, why should we? The food crisis is over; AWS is back and we got the engines that will take us to the stars. I'd say everybody's happy."

Behind them, the 3D-vid sprang to life. Although the image it projected was strangely flat, the scene was familiar.

A woman wearing epaulettes stood with her hands on her hips. The camera jounced and jogged, giving a close up of her feet as a voice-over announced: "Our apologies for the poor quality of the transmission. The following was recorded using old-style two-dimensional mini-cams. Now here with rest of the day's events is . . ."